D1130778

THE LAST TOWN

Center Point
Large Print

Also by Blake Crouch and available from
Center Point Large Print:

Pines
Wayward

THE LAST TOWN

BOOK THREE OF THE WAYWARD PINES SERIES

BLAKE CROUCH

CENTER POINT LARGE PRINT
THORNDIKE, MAINE

This Center Point Large Print edition
is published in the year 2018 by arrangement with
Amazon Publishing, www.apub.com.

The text of this Large Print edition is unabridged.
In other aspects, this book may vary
from the original edition.
Printed in the United States of America
on permanent paper.
Set in 16-point Times New Roman type.

ISBN: 978-1-68324-806-4

Library of Congress Cataloging-in-Publication Data

Names: Crouch, Blake, author.
Title: The last town / Blake Crouch.
Description: Center Point Large Print edition. | Thorndike, Maine :
    Center Point Large Print, 2018. | Series: The Wayward Pines series ;
    book 3
Identifiers: LCCN 2018009467 | ISBN 9781683248064
    (hardcover : alk. paper)
Subjects: LCSH: Secret service—United States—Fiction. |
    Despotism—Fiction. | Large type books. | GSAFD: Suspense fiction.
Classification: LCC PS3603.R68 L37 2018 | DDC 813/.6—dc23
LC record available at https://lccn.loc.gov/2018009467

For my angels, Annslee and Adeline

ABOUT *THE LAST TOWN*

Welcome to Wayward Pines, the last town.

Secret Service agent Ethan Burke arrived in Wayward Pines, Idaho, three weeks ago. In this town, people are told who to marry, where to live, where to work. Their children are taught that David Pilcher, the town's creator, is god. No one is allowed to leave; even asking questions can get you killed.

But Ethan has discovered the astonishing secret of what lies beyond the electrified fence that surrounds Wayward Pines and protects it from the terrifying world beyond. It is a secret that has the entire population completely under the control of a madman and his army of followers, a secret that is about to come storming through the fence to wipe out this last, fragile remnant of humanity.

Blake Crouch's electrifying conclusion to the Wayward Pines Series—a Major Television Event Series in Summer 2014 on FOX—will have you glued to the page right down to the very last word.

Then the Lord spoke to Job out of the storm.

He said: "Who is this that obscures my plans with words without knowledge? Brace yourself like a man; I will question you, and you shall answer me.

"Where were you when I laid the earth's foundation? Tell me, if you understand. Who marked off its dimensions? Surely you know! Who stretched a measuring line across it? On what were its footings set, or who laid its cornerstone—while the morning stars sang together and all the angels shouted for joy?"

JOB 38:1–7 (NIV)

**WE ARE THE LAST OF OUR KIND, A COLONY OF HUMAN BEINGS FROM THE EARLY TWENTY-FIRST CENTURY.
WE LIVE IN THE MOUNTAINS OF WHAT WAS ONCE IDAHO, IN A TOWN CALLED WAYWARD PINES.
OUR COORDINATES ARE 44 DEGREES, 13 MINUTES, 0 SECONDS NORTH, AND 114 DEGREES, 56 MINUTES, 16 SECONDS WEST.
IS ANYBODY OUT THERE?**

—Portion of a voice and Morse code radio transmission broadcast across all short wave bands out of Wayward Pines super structure on a continuous loop for the last eleven years.

PRELUDE

DAVID PILCHER

SUPERSTRUCTURE
WAYWARD PINES
FOURTEEN YEARS AGO

He opens his eyes.

Frigid.

Shivering.

Head throbbing.

Someone stands over him wearing a surgical mask, face a blur.

He doesn't know where he is or, for that matter, who he is.

A clear mask is lowered to his mouth.

The voice—a woman's—urges him, "Take a long, deep breath, and keep breathing in."

The gas he inhales is warm, concentrated oxygen. It flows down his windpipe and hits his lungs with a welcome burst of heat. Though her mouth is covered, the woman leaning over him is smiling at him with her eyes.

"Better?" she asks.

He nods. Her face grows sharper. And her voice . . . Something familiar there.

Not the timbre itself, but the way he feels toward it. Protective. Almost paternal.

"Does your head hurt?" she asks.

He nods.

"That'll pass soon. I know you're feeling a lot of disorientation."

Nod.

"That's completely normal. Do you know where you are?"

Headshake.

"Do you know who you are?"

Headshake.

"That's okay too. You've only had blood in your veins for thirty-five minutes. It usually takes a couple of hours to find your bearings."

He stares up at the lights overhead: long fluorescents, far too bright.

He opens his mouth.

"Don't try to talk yet. Would you like me to explain what's happening?"

Nod.

"Your name is David Pilcher."

He thinks that piece of information sounds right. The name feels like his own on a level he can't quite grasp—at the very least, like a star that belongs in his sky.

"You're not in a hospital. You haven't been in a car accident or suffered a heart attack. Nothing like that."

He wants to say that he can't move. That he feels as cold as death and afraid.

She continues. "You've just come out of suspended animation. Your vitals are all in the green. You've been sleeping for eighteen hundred years in one of a thousand suspension units, which you created. We're all so excited. Your experiment worked. The crew came through at a ninety-seven percent survival rate. Better by a few points than you projected, and with no critical losses. Congratulations."

Pilcher lies on the gurney, blinking at the lights.

The heart monitor he's attached to begins to beep faster and faster, but it isn't from fear or stress.

It's exhilaration.

Within five seconds, it all clicks in.

Who he is.

Where he is.

Why he is.

Like a camera racking focus.

Pilcher reaches a hand up—heavy as a chunk of granite—and pulls the mask away from his mouth. He stares up at the nurse. For the first time in nearly two millennia, he speaks, raspy but clear: "Has anyone gone outside?"

She removes her mask. It's Pam. Twenty

years old and ghost-like in the wake of her long, long sleep.

And yet . . . still so very beautiful.

She smiles. "You know I wouldn't let that happen, David. We waited for you."

Six hours later, Pilcher is on his feet and moving unsteadily down the Level 1 corridor, flanked by Ted Upshaw, Pam, Arnold Pope, and a man named Francis Leven. Leven's official title is "steward" of the superstructure, and he's talking a mile a minute.

". . . had one hull breach in the ark seven hundred eighty-three years ago, but the vacuum sensors caught it."

Pilcher says, "So our provisions—"

"I'm running a battery of tests, but everything appears to have come through fully preserved."

"How much of the crew has been awakened?"

"Only eight, counting us."

They reach the automatic glass doors that open into the five-million-square-foot cavern that serves as a warehouse for provisions and building supplies. Affectionately called "the ark," it is one of the great feats of human engineering and ambition.

A damp, mineralized smell pervades.

Massive globe lights hang down from the ceiling, stretching back into the ark as far as the eye can see.

They walk toward a Humvee parked at the entrance to a tunnel, and already Pilcher is breathless, his legs threatening to seize up with cramps.

Pope drives.

The tunnel's fluorescent luminaries aren't yet operational, and the Humvee plunges down the steep, fifteen-percent grade into abject darkness, nothing to light its way but the lonely headlights blazing off the wet rock walls.

Pilcher rides up front beside his henchman.

The disorientation is still present, but retreating.

His people have told him that the suspension lasted eighteen hundred years, but with each breath he takes, that seems less and less possible. In truth, it feels as though only hours have passed since that New Year's Eve party in 2013, when he and his entire crew drank Dom Pérignon, stripped naked, and climbed into their suspension pods.

His ears release pressure as they descend.

His stomach tingles with nervous energy.

Glancing over his shoulder, Pilcher stares at Leven in the backseat—a lithe young man with the face of a baby but the eyes of a sage.

"We're going to be safe breathing in this atmosphere?" Pilcher asks.

"It has altered," Leven says, "but only slightly. Nitrogen and oxygen, thank God, are still the main components. But the makeup is now one percent more oxygen, one percent less nitrogen. Greenhouse gases have returned to pre–Industrial Age levels."

"I trust you've already begun to depressurize the superstructure?"

"That was the first order of business. We're already sucking in air from outside."

"Any other pertinent bits?"

"It'll be a few days until our systems are fully powered up and debugged."

"Where does our electron clock place us in terms of the Christian calendar?"

"Today is February 14, 3813, in the year of our Lord." Leven grins. "Happy Valentine's Day, all."

Arnold Pope brings the Humvee to a full stop, its high beams shining against the back side of the titanium portal that has protected the tunnel, the superstructure, and all who sleep within from the world outside.

Pope kills the engine, leaves the lights running.

As they all step out of the truck, Pope walks around to the back and opens the cargo doors.

He takes a pump-action shotgun off the rack.

"For God's sake, Arnie," Pilcher says. "Always the pessimist."

"That's why you pay me the big bucks, right? If it were up to me, I'd have my entire security team rolling with us."

"No, we're keeping this intimate for now."

Leven says, "Pam, would you mind bringing your flashlight over?"

As she shines the beam onto the release wheel, Pilcher says, "Let's just wait a beat."

Leven straightens.

Pope heads over.

Ted and Pam turn to face him.

Pilcher's voice is still gravelly from the drugs that revived him.

He says, "Let's not let this moment pass us by." His people study him. "Do you all understand what we've done? We just completed the most dangerous, daring journey in human history. Not across distance. Across time. You know what waits on the other side of this door?"

He lets the question hang.

No one bites.

"Pure discovery."

"I don't follow," Pam says.

"I've said it before, I'll say it again. This is Neil Armstrong going down the steps of Apollo 11 to stand on the moon for the first time. The Wright brothers testing their flyer at Kitty Hawk. Columbus walking ashore into the New World. There's no telling what lies on the other side of this portal."

"You predicted that humanity would become extinct," Pam says.

"Yes, but my prediction was just that. A prediction. I could've been wrong. There could be ten-thousand-foot sky-scrapers out there. Imagine a man in 213 AD stepping into 2013. 'The most beautiful thing we can experience is the mysterious.' Albert Einstein said that. We should all savor this moment."

Leven turns his attention to the release wheel, which he begins to crank counterclockwise.

When it finally locks into place, he says, "Sir? Care to do the honors?"

Pilcher approaches the portal.

Leven says, "It's this latch, right here."

Pilcher throws the latch.

For a moment, nothing happens.

The lights of the Humvee cut out.

Only the beam of Pam's meager flashlight cuts through the darkness.

Something under their feet begins to groan, like an old ship creaking.

The heavy portal door shudders and begins to creak open.

And then . . .

Light spills across the pavement, spreading toward them in a radiant stain.

Pilcher's heart is pounding.

It is the most thrilling moment of his life.

Snow whisks inside across the pavement, and a shot of bone-chilling cold knifes into the tunnel. Pilcher squints against the light.

When the four-foot portal is fully open, it frames the world beyond like a picture.

They all see a boulder-strewn pine forest in the midst of a snowstorm.

They move into the forest, tracking through a foot of soft powder.

It is beyond quiet.

The sound of falling snow like a whisper.

After two hundred yards, Pilcher stops. The others stop too.

He says, "I think this is where the road into Wayward Pines used to be."

They're still standing in a dense pine wood, no sign of a road anywhere.

Pilcher pulls out a compass.

They head north into the valley.

Pines tower above them.

"I wonder," Pilcher says, "how many times this forest burned and regrew."

He's cold. His legs ache. He's certain the others feel the same weakness, but no one complains.

They trudge on until the trees break. How far they've come, he can't be sure. The snow has let up, and, for the first time, he sees something familiar— those massive cliff walls that almost two thousand years ago surrounded the hamlet of Wayward Pines.

It surprises him how much comfort he finds in seeing these mountains again. Two millennia is a long time when it comes to forests and rivers, but the cliffs look virtually unchanged. Like old friends.

Soon, their party is standing in the dead center of the valley.

There's not a single building left.

Not even ruins.

Leven says, "It's like the town was never even here."

"What does this mean?" Pam asks.

"What does what mean?" Pilcher says.

"That nature has taken back over. That the town is gone."

"Impossible to say. Maybe Idaho is now a huge preserve. Maybe Idaho doesn't exist anymore. We have a lot to learn about this new world."

Pilcher looks for Pope. The man has wandered twenty yards away into a clearing, where he kneels down over the snow.

"What is it, Arnie?"

He waves Pilcher over.

As the group gathers around Pope, he points down at a set of tracks.

"Human?" Pilcher asks.

"They're the size of a man's footprint, but the spacing is all wrong."

"How so?"

"Whatever this thing is, it was moving on four limbs. See?" He touches the snow. "Here are the hind legs. There are the forelegs. Look at the distance between tracks. That's one helluva gait."

25

• • •

In the southwest corner of the valley, they find a collection of stones poking up through the ground, scattered through a grove of scrub oak and aspen trees. Pilcher squats down to inspect one of the stones, brushing the snow away from the base. Once a block of polished marble, time has worn it rough.

"What are these?" Pam asks, running her hand across the top of another similar stone.

"The ruins of a cemetery," Pilcher says. "The etchings have been eroded. This is all that's left of twenty-first-century Wayward Pines."

They walk home, back toward the superstructure.

Everyone weak.

Everyone cold.

The snow picks up again, a shroud of white falling against the backdrop of cliffs and evergreens.

"Doesn't particularly feel like anyone's home," Leven says.

"One of the first things we'll do," Pilcher says, "is send out the drones. We'll fly them to Boise, Missoula, even Seattle. We'll know if there's anything left."

They follow their own tracks back into the woods. As a silence descends on the group, a scream rises up in the valley behind them—frail and haunting, echoing off the snow-hidden peaks.

Everyone stops.

Another scream answers—lower in pitch, but containing that same mix of sadness and aggression.

Pope opens his mouth to speak when a veritable nation of screams rises up out of the woods all around them.

They hurry through the snow, jogging at first, but as the screams close in, everyone accelerates to a full-on sprint.

A hundred yards out from the tunnel, Pilcher's legs are finished and sweat pours down his face. The others have reached the portal. They're climbing through, shouting at him to run faster, their voices commingling with the shrieks behind him.

His vision blurs.

He glances back.

Glimpses movement in the pines—pale forms pursuing him on all fours through the trees.

He's gasping for air, thinking, I'm going to die my first day out of suspension.

The world goes black, and his face is suddenly freezing.

He hasn't lost consciousness.

He's just facedown in the snow, unable to move.

As the approaching screams grow louder, he's suddenly hoisted out of the powder. From his new vantage point, draped over Arnold Pope's shoulder, he sees the woods joggling behind him and humanoid creatures bearing down, the closest within fifty feet.

Pope shoves him through the titanium door, and as Pilcher crashes to the floor, Pope scrambles inside.

Pilcher's face presses against the cold concrete.

Pope shouts, "Get back! It's gonna be close!"

The portal slams home.

On the other side, a series of dull thuds crashes into the metal.

Safe now, Pilcher's consciousness is ebbing.

The last thing he hears before slipping under is Pam's voice cutting through the hysteria, shouting, "What the fuck are those things?"

I

TWO HOURS AFTER ETHAN BURKE'S REVELATION

JENNIFER ROCHESTER

The house was so damn dark.

Jennifer tried the kitchen light out of instinct, but nothing happened.

She felt her way around the fridge to the cabinet over the stove, opened it, and grabbed the crystal candlestick holder, a candle, and the box of matches. She turned on the gas and struck a match to the back burner and set the teakettle over the hissing blue flame.

Lighting what was left of the candle, she sat down at the breakfast table.

In her life before, she'd been a pack-a-day smoker, and God could she use a cigarette right now—something to steady her nerves and her hands, which wouldn't stop trembling.

As her eyes filled with tears, the candlelight fractured.

All she could think of was her husband, Teddy, and how far apart she felt from him.

Two thousand years apart to be exact.

She'd always harbored hope that the world was still out there. Beyond the fence. Beyond this nightmare. That her husband was still out there. Her home. Her job at the university. On some level, it was that hope that had gotten her by all these years. Hope that one day she might wake up back in Spokane. Teddy would be lying beside her, still sleeping, and this place—Wayward Pines—would all have been a dream. She would slip quietly out of bed and go into the kitchen and cook him eggs. Brew a pot of strong coffee. She would be waiting for him at the breakfast table when he stumbled out of bed in that disgusting robe, disheveled and sleepy and everything she loved. She'd say, "I had the strangest dream last night," but as she'd try to explain it, all that she'd experienced in Wayward Pines would slip back into the fog of forgotten dreams.

She'd just smile across the table at her husband and say, "I lost it."

Now, her hope was gone.

The loneliness was staggering.

But underneath it simmered anger.

Anger that this had been done to her.

Rage at all the loss.

The teakettle began to whistle.

She struggled to her feet, her mind racing.

Lifting the kettle off the flame, the whistling died away, and she poured the boiling water into her favorite ceramic mug in which she kept a tea infuser perpetually filled with chamomile leaves. Tea in one hand, candle in the other, she moved out of the dark kitchen and into the hallway.

Most of the town was still down at the theater, reeling from the sheriff's revelation, and maybe she should've stayed with everyone else; but the truth of it was that she wanted to be alone. Tonight, she just needed to cry in bed. If sleep came, great, but she wasn't exactly expecting it.

She turned the corner at the bannister and started up the creaking stairs, candlelight flickering across the walls. The power had gone out several times before, but she couldn't escape the feeling that tonight of all nights meant something.

The fact that she'd locked every door and every window gave her some small—very small— peace of mind.

SHERIFF ETHAN BURKE

Ethan stared up at twenty-five feet of steel pylons and spiked conductors wrapped in coils of razor wire. The fence usually hummed with enough current to electrocute a person one thousand times over. So loud you could hear it a hundred yards away and feel it in your fillings at close proximity.

Tonight, Ethan heard nothing.

Worse still, the thirty-foot gate stood wide open.

Locked open.

Shreds of mist skirted past like the front edge of an approaching storm, and Ethan gazed out into the black woods beyond the fence. Over the pounding of his heart, he heard shrieks beginning to echo in the forest.

The abbies were on their way.

David Pilcher's final words to him were set on repeat.

Hell is coming to you.

This was Ethan's fault.

Hell is coming to you.

He'd made the mistake of calling that psychofuck's bluff.

Hell is coming to you.

And telling people the truth.

And now everyone in town, his wife and son included, was going to die.

36

Ethan sprinted back through the forest, the panic growing with every stride, every desperate breath. He weaved between the pines, now running alongside the quiet fence.

His Bronco lay just ahead and already the screams were louder, closer.

Jumping in behind the wheel, he cranked the engine and sped off into the trees, pushing the suspension package to the limit and jarring the last few jags of glass out of what was left of the windshield.

He reached the road that looped back into town and roared up the embankment, back onto pavement.

Pinned the gas pedal to the floorboard.

The engine wailed.

He shot out of the trees and raced beside a pasture.

High beams blazed across the billboard at the edge of town, showing a family of four waving, smiling those carefree 1950s shit-eating grins over the slogan:

WELCOME TO WAYWARD PINES
WHERE PARADISE IS HOME

Not anymore, Ethan thought.

If they were lucky, the abbies would reach the dairy first, slaughtering their way through the cattle before tearing into town.

There it was.

Straight ahead.

The outskirts of Wayward Pines.

On a clear day, the town defined perfection. Neat blocks of brightly colored Victorian houses. White picket fences. Lush, green grass. Main Street looked like something built for tourists to wander down and dream of retiring here to live the good life. The quaint life. The mountain walls that surrounded the town promised shelter and security. At first blush, nothing about it felt like a place you couldn't leave—a place where you'd be killed for even trying.

Except tonight.

Tonight, the houses and buildings stood ominously dark.

Ethan turned onto Tenth Avenue and screamed through seven blocks before ripping out onto Main so hard the right-side wheels lifted off the ground.

Up ahead, at the intersection of Main and Eighth, the entire town stood where he'd left them—out in front of the opera house. Four hundred and something souls waiting around in the dark like they'd been kicked out of a ball en masse, still dressed in their ridiculous costumes from the fête.

Ethan shut off the car and climbed out.

It was eerie to see Main Street in the dark, all that storefront glass lit only by torchlight.

There was the Steaming Bean.

Wooden Treasures—Kate and Harold Ball-ingers' toy store.

The Wayward Pines Hotel.

Richardson's Bakery.

The Biergarten.

The Sweet Tooth.

Wayward Pines Realty Associates, where Ethan's wife, Theresa, worked.

The noise of the crowd was overwhelming.

People were emerging from their disbelief and shock in the wake of Ethan's decision to tell them all the truth about Wayward Pines. Beginning to talk to one another, in some ways, for the first time.

Kate Ballinger hurried over. It was Kate and her husband, Harold, who'd been on the execution block for tonight's fête, whose lives Ethan's revelation had momentarily saved. Somebody had done a fast-stitch job on the gash above her left eye, but her face was still streaked with blood, which had also matted her prematurely white hair. Kate's disappearance in Wayward Pines had brought Ethan to this town two thousand years ago. In another lifetime, they had worked together in the Secret Service. They'd been partners. For a brief, scorching window, they'd been more than partners.

Ethan took Kate by the arm and hustled her around to the back of the Bronco, out of earshot from the crowd. She'd almost died tonight, and as Ethan stared down at her, he could see in her eyes that she was holding everything together by a fraying thread.

He said, "Pilcher killed the power."

"I know."

"No, I mean he killed the power to the fence as well. He opened the gate."

She studied Ethan, as if trying to process exactly how bad a piece of news she'd just received.

"So those things . . ." she said. "The aberrations . . ."

"They can walk right into town now. And they're coming. I heard them at the fence."

"How many?"

"I don't know. Even a small group would be catastrophic."

Kate glanced back at the crowd.

The conversations were dying out, people edging closer to hear the news.

"Some of us have weapons," she said. "A few have machetes."

"That's not going to cut it."

"Can't you reason with Pilcher? Call him back? Change his mind?"

"We're past that point."

"Then we get everyone back inside the opera house," she said. "There are no windows. Just one exit on either side of the stage. Double doors leading in. We'll barricade ourselves inside."

"What if we're under siege for days? No food. No heat. No water. And there's no amount of barricading that will keep the abbies out indefinitely."

"Then what, Ethan?"

"I don't know, but we can't just send people back to their homes."

"Some have already gone."

"I told you to keep everyone here."

"I tried."

"How many went home?"

"Fifty, sixty."

"Jesus."

Ethan spotted Theresa and Ben—his precious family—moving toward him through the crowd.

He said, "If I can get into the superstructure, if I can show Pilcher's inner circle who the man they serve really is, then we might have a chance."

"So go. Right now."

"I'm not leaving my family. Not like this. Not without a real plan."

Theresa reached him. She'd pulled her long blonde hair into a ponytail, and both she and Ben were dressed in dark clothing.

Ethan kissed her, then ruffled Ben's hair. Ethan could already see the man his twelve-year-old boy might become shining through his eyes. Maturity threatening.

"What did you find?" Theresa asked him.

"Nothing good."

"I've got it," Kate said. "We need to be somewhere safe while you break into the super-structure."

"Right."

"Somewhere protected. Defendable. Already stockpiled with provisions."

"Exactly."

She smiled. "I might actually know of a place like that."

Ethan said, "The Wanderers' cavern."

"Yeah."

"That might work. I have guns at the sheriff's station."

"Go get them. Take Brad Fisher with you." She pointed to the sidewalk. "He's right over there."

"How are we going to get this many people up the cliff?"

"I'll separate everyone into groups of a hundred," Kate said, "with each group led by someone who knows the way."

"What do we do about the ones who went home?" Theresa asked.

She was answered with a single, distant scream.

The crowd had been murmuring.

Now everyone went silent.

The sound had come from south of town—a fragile, malignant moan.

Nothing that could be explained or described, because you didn't just hear it.

You *felt* its meaning.

And its meaning was this: *hell is coming*.

Ethan said, "It's going to be hard enough to protect the people who stayed."

"So they're just on their own?"

"We're all on our own now."

He went around to the front passenger seat of the Bronco, reached in, and grabbed the bullhorn. Handing it to Kate, he asked, "You got this?"

She nodded.

Ethan looked at Theresa. "I want you and Ben to stay with Kate."

"Okay."

Ben said, "I'm coming with you, Dad."

"I need you with Mom."

"But I can help you."

"*This* is how you help me." Ethan turned to Kate. "I'll catch up after the sheriff's office."

"Come to the little park at the north end of town."

"With the gazebo?"

"That's the one."

Brad Fisher, Wayward Pines's only lawyer, sat awkwardly in the destroyed front passenger seat of Ethan's Bronco, clutching the handle on the door as Ethan hit sixty on First Avenue.

Ethan glanced over. "Where's your wife?"

Brad said, "We were in the theater. You were

talking, telling us everything. Then I looked over and Megan was just gone."

Ethan said, "Considering what she was teaching the children behind their parents' backs, she probably figured people would see her as a traitor. Feared for her life. How do you feel about her now?"

This seemed to catch Brad off guard. Normally, he was spit-shined and clean-shaven, the model of a competent young lawyer. Now, he scratched at the sandpaper on his chin.

"I don't know. I never really felt like I knew her or that she knew me. We lived together because we were told to. We slept in the same bed. Sometimes we slept together."

"Sounds like a lot of real marriages. Did you love her?"

Brad sighed. "It's complicated. You did the right thing, by the way. Telling us."

"If I'd known he'd kill the power to the fence—"

"Don't go there, Ethan. You can't play that game. You did what you believed was right. You saved Kate and Harold. Showed us all what our lives are really worth."

"I wonder," Ethan said, "how long that sentiment is going to last once people start dying."

The high beams fired across the dark sheriff's station. Ethan steered over the curb and took the

Bronco right up the sidewalk. He brought it to a stop a few feet from the entrance and climbed out, clicking on a flashlight as he and Brad reached the double doors. Ethan unlocked them, propped one open.

"What are we grabbing?" Brad asked as they ran through the lobby and turned down the corridor to Ethan's office.

"Anything that shoots."

Brad manned the flashlight as Ethan pulled guns out of the cabinet and matched up the ammunition.

He set a Mossberg 930 on the desk and pushed in eight slugs.

Fed thirty rounds into the magazine of a Bushmaster AR-15.

Topped off the mag for his Desert Eagle.

There were more shotguns.

Hunting rifles.

Glocks.

A sig.

A .357 Smith & Wesson.

He got two more handguns loaded, but it was all costing too much time.

KATE HEWSON BALLINGER

She grabbed hold of Harold's arm. Her husband was taking his group to an entrance a few blocks south, and she was leading hers to the north end of town.

She threw her arms around his neck, kissed him long and deep.

"I love you," she said.

He grinned, his silver hair sweat-plastered to his forehead despite the chill, the bruises on his face beginning to blacken.

"Katie, if something happens—"

"Don't do that," she said.

"What?"

"Just get your ass to the cliff."

Several blocks away, something howled. As she moved toward the crowd of people waiting to follow her to safety, she glanced back and blew Harold a kiss.

He snatched it out of the air.

JENNIFER

In her bedroom, Jennifer set the candle on the dresser and stripped out of the costume she'd worn to the fête—a black trench coat over red long underwear, topped off with a homemade pair of devil's horns. Her nightgown waited for her, hanging on the back of the door.

Once in bed, she drank her chamomile tea and watched the candlelight dance across the ceiling.

The tea went down warm.

This had been her routine going on three years now, and she thought it had been wise not to break it tonight. When your world falls apart, cling to the familiar.

She thought of all the other residents of Wayward Pines.

They'd be going through some version of this.

Questioning all they'd been told.

Coming to terms with how grievously they'd been wronged.

What would tomorrow bring?

The window beside her bed was cracked, a stream of chill night air trickling in. She kept her room cold by choice, loving the feel of sleeping in a freezing room under a mountain of blankets.

Through the glass, it was absolutely dark.

The crickets had gone silent.

She set her mug of tea on the bedside table and pulled the blankets up over her legs. There was only a half inch left of the candle on her dresser, and she didn't really want to be in total darkness just yet.

Let it burn out on its own.

She shut her eyes.

Felt like she was falling.

So many thoughts, so much fear pressing in.

A tangible weight.

Just sleep.

She thought of Teddy. This last year, she'd found herself remembering his smell, his tone of voice, what his hands had felt like on her body, far clearer than her memory of his face.

She was forgetting what he looked like.

Somewhere out in the darkness, a man began to scream.

Jennifer straightened.

She'd never heard screaming like this.

Horror and disbelief and incomprehensible agony all compressed into a single outburst that seemed to go on and on and on.

This was the sound of someone being killed.

Had they gone ahead with Kate and Harold's execution anyway?

The screaming stopped like a spigot had been turned off.

Jennifer looked down.

She was on her feet, standing on the cold hardwood floor.

She went to the window, raised it several inches higher.

Cold flooded in.

Someone shouted inside a house nearby.

A door slammed.

Somebody sprinted through the alley.

Another scream echoed through the valley, but this one was different. It was the same sound that monster had made inside the sheriff's Bronco.

A god-awful, inhuman shriek.

Other screams answered as a strong, pungent smell—like rotten musk—pushed into the bedroom, riding on the breeze.

A low, throaty growl started down in her garden.

Jennifer closed her window and threw the lock.

She stumbled back, and as she sat down on the mattress, something came through the living-room window downstairs.

Jennifer jerked her head toward the door.

The candle flame on the dresser winked out.

She let out a gasp.

The room was pitch black, her hand invisible in front of her face.

She jumped to her feet and staggered toward the bedroom door, banged her knee on a hope chest at the foot of the bed, but managed to stay on her feet.

She reached the door.

Heard the steps creaking as something came up the staircase.

Jennifer eased the door shut and felt around for the lock.

It clicked into the housing.

Whatever had broken into her house was now out in the hallway, the floorboards groaning under its weight.

More noise downstairs.

Clicks and screeches filling the house.

She got down on her hands and knees and crawled across the floor as the footsteps outside her door drew closer. Flattening herself, she squeezed under the bed, her heart pounding against the dusty hardwood floor.

She could hear more of them climbing the stairs.

The door to her bedroom exploded off the hinges.

The footsteps of whatever entered her bedroom made a clicking sound on the hardwood. Like claws.

Or talons.

She smelled it, stronger than ever, a potpourri of dead things—rot and blood and an otherworldly stench beyond her understanding.

She didn't make a sound.

By the side of the bed, the floorboards cracked, as if with the weight of something kneeling down.

She held her breath.

Something hard and smooth grazed her arm.

She screamed and pulled back.

Her shoulder suddenly felt cold.

She put her hand to it.

It came away wet. She'd been cut by something.

Whispered, "Please God . . ."

There were others in the room now.

Oh, Teddy. She just wanted to see his face. One last time. If this was really the end.

The bed lifted, one of the legs scraping across her side as it crashed into the wall.

In total darkness, she couldn't move, paralyzed with fear. Her shoulder bled profusely but she couldn't feel a thing, her body gone numb, mechanical, as the fight-or-flight response kicked in.

They were near her now, standing over her, their alien respirations fast and shallow, like panting dogs.

She put her head between her knees in the brace position.

Two weeks before they'd come on their fateful trip to Wayward Pines, she and Teddy had spent a Saturday at Riverfront Park in Spokane. Thrown a picnic blanket down in the grass and stayed until dusk, reading their books and watching the white water spill over the falls.

And for a second, she captured his face. Not straight on, but from the side. Late sunlight fringing what hair he had left, glinting off the wire-rimmed glasses. He was watching the sun go down over the falls. Content. In the moment. And she had been too.

Teddy.

He turned to look at her.

Smiling.

As the end came.

ETHAN

Brad was shoving the ammo-laden rucksack through the busted back window as Ethan jumped in behind the wheel.

He checked his watch.

They'd burned eleven minutes.

"Let's go!" Ethan said.

Brad yanked the door open and climbed onto the broken seat.

Headlights blazed through the glass doors into the lobby of the sheriff's station.

Ethan glanced in the rearview mirror. Through the reddish glow of the taillights, a pale form streaked past.

He shifted into reverse.

They backed down the sidewalk and Ethan's head hit the ceiling as the tires launched off the curb.

Ethan braked hard, brought it to a dead stop in the middle of the road, and shifted into drive.

Something struck the passenger-side door, Brad screamed, and by the time Ethan looked over, Brad's legs were already sliding through the empty window frame.

Ethan couldn't see the blood in the dark, but he could smell it—a strong, sudden waft of rust in the air.

He pulled his pistol.

The screams had gone silent.

All he could hear was the fading scrape of Brad's shoes dragging across the pavement.

Ethan grabbed the flashlight, which Brad had dropped between the seats.

Shined it out into the street.

Oh my God.

The beam struck an abby.

It was crouched on its hind legs over Brad, its face buried in his throat.

It looked up, mouth blood-dark, and hissed at the light with the venomous warning of a wolf protecting its kill.

Behind it, the light showed more pale figures coming down the middle of the street.

Ethan punched the gas.

In the rearview mirror, a dozen abbies chased the car on all fours. The one out in front came up alongside his door. It leapt at Ethan's window, just missed, hit the side of the car instead, and bounced off.

Ethan watched it tumble across the street as he forced the pedal to the floor.

When he looked back through the windshield, a small abby stood twenty feet ahead of the grille, frozen in the headlights, teeth bared.

Ethan braced.

At contact, the bumper blasted the abby straight back thirty feet. He ran it over and dragged it for half a block, the Bronco jarring so violently he could barely keep his grip on the steering wheel.

The undercarriage finally spit it out.

Ethan raced north.

The rearview mirror showed a dark, empty street.

He breathed again.

Near the north end of town, Ethan turned west, headed several blocks toward Main until the headlights swiped across a line of people in the street, faces lit by a handful of torches.

He steered the Bronco over the curb.

Left the keys in the ignition so the lights would keep burning.

He went around to the back of the Bronco, lowered the tailgate, and grabbed one of the three loaded shotguns.

Kate was standing beside an open trapdoor behind a bench, its underside constructed of one-by-four planks and rusted hinges, the top camouflaged with dirt and grass. She and another man were lowering people, one by one, underground.

Their eyes met as he approached.

He shoved a shotgun into her hands and looked back at the crowd—still twenty-five or thirty left to go.

"They need to be underground five minutes ago," Ethan said.

"Going as fast as we can."

"Where are Ben and Theresa?"

"Already down below."

"The abbies are here, Kate."

He saw the question in her eyes before she asked, "Where's Brad?"

"They got him, and I'm telling you, we have a couple minutes tops and then it's all over."

The crowd was moving with the efficiency of an evacuation—orderly, no one talking, a hushed intensity in the air.

Screams—human and inhuman—were erupting across the town with greater frequency.

Ethan turned to the crowd.

He said, "I have a carful of weapons. If you ever owned firearms in your prior life, if you have any experience or comfort level whatsoever, come with me."

Ten people stepped out of line and followed Ethan over to the back of the Bronco.

Hecter Gaither, the town pianist, stood among them. He was tall and lanky, salt-and-pepper hair with whitewashed wings. Fragile, almost regal features. For the fête, he'd dressed up like a murderous fairy.

Ethan asked, "What'd you shoot in your past life, Hecter?"

"I used to go duck hunting with my father every Christmas morning."

Ethan handed him a Mossberg.

"I loaded this up with twelve-gauge slugs. It's going to kick a bit more than the bird-shot rounds you're used to."

Hecter held it by the stock—so strange to see those soft, dexterous hands clutching a tactical shotgun.

Ethan said, "You and I will go down last. I'll be right there with you." He turned his attention back to the arsenal. "I've got a few revolvers and a handful of semiauto pistols left. Who wants what?"

PILCHER

WAYWARD PINES
TWELVE YEARS AGO

It's morning.

An autumn day.

They didn't make skies this blue in his life before. You can look straight up into purple. The air so clear and clean it suggests a hyperreality, the colors blindingly intense.

Pilcher walks down the road into town. It was paved two weeks ago, and it still reeks of tar.

He passes the new billboard where a worker is painting the "e" in "Paradise." When completed, the phrase will read, "Welcome to Wayward Pines Where Paradise is Home."

Pilcher says, "Good morning! Good work!"

"Thank you, sir!"

The town has a long way yet to go, but the valley is beginning to look almost civilized. The forest has been mostly felled, save for a handful of trees left standing to line the streets and shade front yards.

A concrete truck rumbles past.

In the distance, new houses stand in various stages of completion. The residences were prefabricated prior to suspension. With all the foundations laid, the work seems to be accelerating, the town growing faster each day as homes begin to take shape.

The school is nearly finished.

The bottom three floors of the hospital framed.

Pilcher arrives at the graded, unpaved corner of what will one day be Eighth and Main.

The valley hums with the distant whine of saws and the pressurized bursts of nails shooting into studs.

The buildings that will soon line Main Street are fully framed, their yellow pine boards bright in the early sun.

Arnold Pope drives up in a topless Jeep Wrangler.

Pilcher's right-hand man climbs out of the Jeep and struts over.

"Come down to see the progress?" Pope asks.

"Magnificent, isn't it?"

"We're actually ahead of schedule. If all

goes well, we'll have a hundred seventy homes completed before the snow flies, and the exteriors of all the buildings. Which means we'll be able to continue working on the interiors through the winter."

"So when may I schedule the formal ribbon cutting?"

"Next spring."

Pilcher smiles, imagining it—a warm day in May and the valley popping with blossoms and the baby greens and yellows of new leaves.

A fresh start. Humanity's blank slate.

"Have you considered how you'll explain all of this to the first residents?"

They walk down the middle of the street, Pilcher eyeing the scaffolding fronting the building that will become the opera house.

"I imagine there will be some shock and disbelief at the outset, but once they understand what I've given them the chance to be a part of?"

"They'll fall on the ground thanking you," Pope says.

Pilcher smiles.

A flatbed truck carrying a load of raw lumber rumbles past.

"Can you fathom being given this

opportunity?" Pilcher muses. "In the world we came from, our existence was so easy. And so full of discontent because it was so easy. How do you find meaning when you're one of seven billion? When food, clothing, everything you need is just one Walmart away? When we numb our minds to sleep on all manner of screens and HD entertainment, the meaning of life, of our existence and purpose, becomes lost."

"And what is that?" Pope asks.

"What is what?"

"Our purpose."

"To perpetuate our species of course. To reign over this planet. And we will again. Not in your or my lifetime, but we will. The people I bring out of suspension to populate my town won't have Facebook or iPhones, iPads, Twitter, next-day delivery. They'll interact like our species used to. Face-to-face. And they'll live knowing they're the last of humanity, that outside our fence are a billion monsters that want to devour them. With that knowledge, they'll abide in a full understanding that in the face of these enormous stakes, their lives have taken on incomprehensible worth. And isn't that all we want in the end? To feel useful? Of value?"

Pilcher smiles as his town—his dream—comes to life before his eyes.

He says, "This place is going to be our Eden."

THE TURNERS

Jim Turner kissed his eight-year-old daughter on the forehead and wiped away the tears that were streaming out of her eyes.

She said, "But I want you to stay with us."

"I have to go secure the house."

"I'm scared."

"Mommy's staying with you."

"Why are people screaming outside?"

"I don't know," he lied.

"Is it because of those monsters? We learned about them in school. Mr. Pilcher protects us from them."

"I don't know what they are, Jessica, but I have to go make sure you and Mommy are safe, okay?"

The little girl nodded.

"I love you, sweetheart."

"I love you too, Daddy."

He stood, put his hands on his wife's face. Couldn't see her in the darkness, but he could feel her lips trembling, the wetness of tears running over them.

He said, "You have water, food, a flashlight." He tried to make a joke out of it. "Even a pot to piss in."

She grabbed his neck, put her lips to his ear.

"Don't do this."

"There's no other way and you know it."

"The basement—"

"It won't work. The boards are too long to go across the door." He heard their neighbors, the Millers, dying in their home across the street. "When it comes time to get out—"

"*You'll* break us out."

"I want nothing more. But if I'm not here to do it, use the crowbar. You'll have to wedge it into the jamb."

"We should've stayed with the others."

"I know, but we didn't, and now we're doing the best we can. No matter what you hear in this bedroom, you stay in this closet, and you don't make a sound. Cover her ears if—"

"Don't say that."

"If what, Daddy?"

"Oh God, don't say that."

"I love you, my girls. Now I have to shut this door."

"No, Daddy!"

"Quiet, Jess," he whispered.

Jim Turner kissed his wife.

He kissed his daughter.

Then he shut them into the bedroom closet on the second floor of their lavender-colored Victorian.

His toolbox was already open on the floor.

He flicked on his flashlight and chose a suitable

two-by-four from the pieces of scrap lumber he'd carried in from the shed—remnants of a doghouse he'd built last summer.

Those warm afternoons working in the back-yard . . .

Mrs. Miller's screaming jettisoned the memory into oblivion.

"No-no-no-no-no-no-no! Oh Gooooooooddddd!"

Jessica was crying in the closet, Gracie struggling to comfort her.

Jim grabbed a hammer. He started nails on each end of the board. Screws would have been preferable but there was no time. He held the pine board across the doorframe and drove the nails into the studs.

His mind wouldn't stop.

He kept replaying what the sheriff had said, but he couldn't wrap his head around it.

How could this be all that was left of humanity?

By the time he had four boards nailed across the doorframe, the Millers had gone quiet across the street.

He dropped the hammer, wiped his brow.

Dripping with sweat.

Kneeling down, he put his lips to the closet door.

"Jessica? Gracie?"

"I can hear you," his wife said.

"You're nailed in," Jim said. "Now I have to go find a place to hide."

"Please be safe."

68

He put his hand on the door.

"I love you both so much."

Gracie said something back but he couldn't hear the words. Too muffled. Too faint. Too ruined by tears.

Rising to his feet, he grabbed the flashlight and the hammer—the nearest thing to a weapon in his toolbox.

At the bedroom door, he turned the lock and closed it gently behind him.

The hallway was dark.

The last half hour had been so filled with shouting and shrieks that the silence struck him wrong, like a lie.

Where will you hide?

How will you survive?

He stopped at the top of the staircase. He was tempted to use the light, but feared it might draw attention.

With a hand on the bannister for a guide, he went slowly down the creaking steps. The living room stood in impenetrable shadow. Jim moved to the front door. He'd locked the dead bolt, but he had a feeling that didn't matter. From what he'd seen, these things were running through the windows.

Stay inside?

Go?

On the other side of the door, he heard something scrape.

Leaned into the peephole.

There were no streetlamps working, but he could actually see outside, the pavement and the picket fences and the cars just faintly illuminated by residual starlight.

Three of those *things* were crawling up the flagstones that led from the picket fence to the front door.

He'd caught glimpses of them streaking down the street from his second-floor bedroom window, but he hadn't yet seen one up close.

None of them were larger than he was, but their muscle tone was extraordinary.

They looked—

Like humanity wrapped in the trappings of a monster.

Equipped with talons instead of fingers, teeth designed for cutting and tearing, and they brandished arms that seemed too long in proportion to the rest of their body. Longer even than their legs.

He said under his breath, like a prayer, "What the hell are you?"

They reached the porch.

Fear suddenly wore him like a glove.

He backed away from the door, moving through the dark again, between the sofa and the coffee table, and then into the kitchen, where the starlight filtered through the window over the sink just sufficiently to brighten the linoleum and light the way.

Jim set the hammer on the counter and took the back-door key off the nail beside the door.

Something crashed into the front door as he worked the key into the lock.

A wood-splintering, lock-rattling collision.

He turned the key, the dead bolt retracting.

Ripped open the back door as the front door punched open.

The steps leading up to the second floor, to the bedroom, to the closet where his girls were in hiding would be the first thing those monsters saw.

Jim walked several steps back into the kitchen, and said, "Hey, guys? Over here!"

An eardrum-riving shriek filled the house.

He couldn't see a thing, but he heard those creatures slamming through tables and chairs as they came for him. He tore back through the kitchen, shutting the door after him and launching down the single step into his perfect square of grass.

Past the doghouse.

Toward the fence.

Glass broke behind him.

As he reached the gate that opened into the alley, he glanced back, saw one of those things climbing through the kitchen window as the other two flung themselves into the back door.

He flipped open the hasp and dug his shoulder into the gate.

ETHAN

The shrieks of the abbies were less than a block away as Ethan lowered himself through the opening, grabbed hold of the handle on the underside of the trapdoor, and pulled it closed above him.

The tunnel swelled with the reverberating noise of a hundred voices down below, loud enough to drown out the abbies.

He searched, but there was no lock on this side of the hatch, no method of securing it against the world above.

Ethan descended the ladder, twenty-five rungs down to the floor of a tunnel brimming with the firelight of a dozen torches.

It was a six-by-six culvert of crumbling concrete, broken by roots and vines, and a couple thousand years old. It ran beneath the town, and, aside from the cemetery, it represented the last original construction leftover from twenty-first-century Wayward Pines.

It felt cold and dank and ancient.

People stood single file, their backs against the walls like schoolchildren assembled for some terrifying drill. Tense. Expectant. Shivering. Some wide-eyed, others blank-faced, as if in complete denial of what was happening.

Ethan jogged up the tunnel to Kate.

"Everybody in?" she asked.

"Yeah. Lead the way. Hecter and I will bring up the rear."

As Ethan moved back down the line, he held his finger to his lips, urging silence.

When he passed his wife and son, he caught Theresa's eye and winked, squeezing her hand as he hurried by.

They had already begun to move as he neared the end.

He pulled the last torchbearer out of line. She tended bar at the Biergarten on weekends. Maggie something.

"What do you want me to do?" she asked.

She was young, scared.

Ethan said, "Just hold your light. It's Maggie, right?"

"Yeah."

"I'm Ethan."

"I know."

"Let's go."

The group moved slowly enough as a whole for Ethan, Hecter, and Maggie to backpedal without fear of falling. The torchlight flickered across the crumbling concrete, illuminating an empty stretch of tunnel forty feet behind them, the walls fringed with light, the center space disturbingly black.

There was the sound of footsteps in water, a few hushed voices, and little else.

As they traveled, Ethan's mind wandered to Theresa and Ben. They were only fifty feet away, but he didn't like being any distance from them under these conditions.

They came to a junction.

Maggie's torch momentarily illuminated the intersecting tunnels.

For a split second, Ethan thought he heard screams echoing down through the dark, but they were lost to the sound of his group's passage.

"Are we doing okay?" Maggie asked.

A tremor in her voice.

"Yes," Ethan said. "We'll be safe soon."

"I'm cold."

Her costume for the fête was a bikini under a raincoat, and fur-lined boots.

Ethan said, "We'll have a fire where we're going."

"I'm scared."

"You're doing great, Maggie."

Two junctions later, they hung a right into a new tunnel.

As they passed an old iron ladder that climbed into darkness, Ethan stopped.

"What's that sound?" Hecter asked.

Ethan looked at Maggie. "Let me have your torch."

"Why?"

He grabbed it and handed her his shotgun.

Climbed with one hand on the rungs, one hand gripping the torch.

After ten steps, Hecter's voice reached up from below.

"Ethan, not to complain, but I can't see a thing down here."

"I'll be back in one minute."

"What are you doing?" Maggie called out. There were tears in her voice, but Ethan kept climbing, until his head bumped against the hatch. He clung to the top rung of the ladder, the trapdoor lit by the firelight, the flame warm near his face.

Maggie and Hecter were still calling out to him.

He eased the trapdoor open.

Compared to the tunnel, the starlit town was bright as day.

The noise that had drawn him up the ladder was screaming.

Human screaming.

And what he saw, he didn't know how to process.

How do you make sense of people running down the middle of a street that could've been the cover of a *Saturday Evening Post*, chased by a horde of monsters, pale white, translucent in the night, some sprinting upright, others moving on all fours with a bounding gait like wolves?

You process it piecemeal.

A string of indelible images.

Shrieks from the nearest house as an abby plows through the front window.

Three abbies running down one of the officers of the fête, who stops to face them at the last moment and swings his machete too early, just missing the nose of the lead abby as the other two tackle him to the ground.

Thirty yards away, an abby pulling out loops of intestine and shoveling them into its jaws as the man pinned beneath its talons makes the last noise—awful, desperate screaming—he will ever make.

In the middle of Main Street, a large abby on top of Megan Fisher, violating her.

A dozen bodies already scattered across Main, most lying absolutely still in puddles of their own insides, two barely crawling, three being eaten alive.

Like a horrific game, no one running in any particular direction.

Ethan had the urge to go above ground and help. Save someone. Just one person. Kill just one of those monsters.

But it would be death.

He didn't even have his shotgun.

This group—one quarter of Wayward Pines—had been ambushed en route to their trapdoor.

No weapons save a few machetes. But would it really matter if they'd all been armed? Would it matter for Ethan's group if the abbies discovered the tunnels?

A terrifying thought.

Think about your family.

They're below you right now.

They need you.

They need you alive.

"Ethan!" Maggie shouted. "Come on!"

Above ground, a man shot past, running as hard as Ethan had ever seen someone run, the speed and sheer energy output only attainable by someone in fear of an impending, unthinkable death.

The abby chasing him was on all fours and closing fast, and as the man glanced back, Ethan recognized him as Jim Turner, the town dentist.

A second abby collided with Jim at full speed, the man's neck snapping from the brute force of the impact.

The questions were inescapable—what if Ethan hadn't made this revelation to the town? What if he'd let them kill Kate and Harold, go on with things the way they'd always been? These people would certainly not be dying right now.

Ethan carefully lowered the trapdoor and descended.

Maggie was hysterical below him, Hecter trying to comfort her.

Ethan reached the bottom, traded back the torch for the gun, and said, "Let's go."

They moved quickly up the tunnel, the rest of their group out of sight.

"What was happening up there?" Maggie asked.

Ethan said, "One of the other groups didn't make it underground in time."

Hecter said, "We have to help them."

"There is no helping them."

"What does that mean?" Maggie asked.

Ethan glimpsed a shimmer of torchlight in the distance and quickened his pace.

He said, "We need to focus on getting our people to safety. Nothing else."

"Were people dying?" Maggie asked.

"Yes."

"How many?"

"I imagine all of them eventually."

THE RICHARDSONS

Bob Richardson slid in behind the wheel of his 1982 Oldsmobile Cutlass Ciera and cranked the engine as his wife, Barbara, piled into the front passenger seat beside him.

"This is the stupidest idea," she said.

He put the car into gear and eased out into the dark street.

"What's yours?" he asked. "Wait inside the house for those things to break in?"

"Your lights aren't on," Barbara said.

"That's intentional, darling."

"You don't think they can hear our engine?"

"Will you shut up and let me drive please?"

"Of course. This'll be the shortest trip ever taken on account of there being no roads out of town."

Bob turned onto First Avenue.

He wasn't about to admit it verbally, or by action (which would mean using the lights), but it was pretty dark. Arguably too dark to drive without headlights.

It had been months since he'd been behind the wheel, and he felt rusty.

They passed the sheriff's station.

With their windows rolled up, the screams emanating from town barely intruded into the tense silence inside the car.

Soon, they reached the outskirts.

Through his window, Bob could see movement in the pasture.

"They're out there," Barbara said.

"I know it."

She reached across his lap and hit the lights. Twin beams shot out across the grassland. Eviscerated cows littered the pasture by the dozens, each one surrounded by a cluster of monsters in the throes of gorging themselves.

"Goddammit, Barbara!"

They all looked up from their kills, bloody mouths glistening in the high beams.

Bob floored the accelerator.

They blew past the goodbye sign—a perfect 1950s family, smiling and waving.

WE HOPE YOU ENJOYED YOUR VISIT
TO WAYWARD PINES! DON'T BE A
STRANGER! COME BACK SOON!

The road entered the forest.

Bob downgraded the high beams to corner lamps, the fog lights just bright enough to keep him straddling the double yellow.

Mist swept across the road between the narrow corridor of pines.

Bob kept glancing in the rearview mirror, but all he could see was a tiny swath of scrolling pavement lit red by the taillights.

"Go faster!" Barbara said.

"I can't. There's a hairpin turn coming up."

She climbed between the seats into the back and sat on her knees, staring through the window.

"Anything?" Bob asked.

"No. What are we going to do?"

"I don't know, but at least we aren't in town, in the midst of everything. Maybe we could just pull off into a quiet place in the trees?" he suggested. "Ride this out?"

"What if there's no end to it?" she asked.

The question hung between them like a black cloud.

The road out of town began to curve and Bob steered into it, keeping their speed under twenty miles per hour.

Barbara was crying in the backseat.

"I wish he hadn't told us," she said.

"What are you talking about?"

"Sheriff Burke. This is all happening because he told us the truth."

"You're probably right."

"I'm not saying I loved it here, but you know what?" Barbara sniveled. "I didn't worry about bills. I didn't worry about our mortgage. You and I got to run a bakery."

"You had gotten used to the way of things."

"Exactly."

"But we couldn't talk about our past," Bob

said. "We never saw our friends or family. We were forced to marry."

"That didn't turn out so bad," she said.

Bob held his tongue as he drove through the heart of the curve.

The road out of town became the road into town.

He eased off the gas as they passed the welcome sign.

Wayward Pines lay straight ahead, enveloped in darkness.

He let the car roll to a stop and killed the engine.

"We just wait here?" Barbara asked.

"For now."

"Shouldn't we keep moving?"

"There's barely any gas left."

She climbed back into the front seat.

She said, "People are dying out there. Right now."

"I know."

"That goddamned sheriff."

"I'm glad he did it."

"What?"

"I said I'm glad."

"No, I heard you the first time. I mean, why? Our neighbors are being slaughtered, Bob."

"We were slaves."

"How are you enjoying your new freedom?"

"If this is the end, I'm glad I know the truth."

"You're not scared?"

"I'm terrified."

Bob opened his door.

"Where are you going?" Barbara asked. The interior dome light burned his eyes.

"I need a moment alone."

"I'm not getting out of this car."

"That's kind of the point, darling."

ETHAN

As they closed in on their group, Ethan registered the growing disconnect between what he'd seen above ground and the fact that his people were still alive down here in the tunnel. It reminded him of the sickening, random way that fate and chance figured into battle—if you had stepped left instead of right, the bullet would have gone through your eye instead of your friend's. If Kate had led their group to a different tunnel entrance, it could've been Ethan and his family being slaughtered on Main Street. He was having an impossible time putting Megan Fisher out of his mind. He'd seen enough death and destruction in Iraq to know that it would be poor Megan who would haunt his dreams for many nights to come. Knew he would always wonder—what if he'd risked everything and gone outside? What if he'd killed her attacker? Saved her? Carried her back to the tunnel? He would play that scene over and over until it bulked up with the perfection of a fantasy. Anything to replace the image of that woman under the abby in the middle of the road. There were still moments from the war he carried and would always carry—incomprehensible agony and suffering.

This trumped them all.

They reached the end of the line just as the group was turning up a new tunnel.

Ethan thinking, *One quarter of humanity was just wiped out.*

He looked down the line of his people, saw the back of Theresa's head in the low light.

The need to be close to her and Ben was overwhelming.

Megan in the street.

Stop.

Megan screaming.

Stop.

Megan—

A single, piercing howl blasted through the tunnel.

Maggie and Hecter stopped.

Ethan raised his shotgun.

The torch began to shake violently in Maggie's hand.

Ethan glanced back.

The line had stalled—everyone had heard, everyone craning their necks, straining to stare down into the darkness of the tunnel.

Ethan said to everyone, "Keep the line moving. Don't stop no matter what. Just go."

They went on.

After fifty feet, Maggie said, "I think I hear something."

"What?" Hecter asked.

"It's like . . . splashing. Someone walking through the water."

"That's just our group."

She shook her head and pointed into the darkness. "It's coming from that direction."

Ethan said, "Hold up. Let everybody get ahead of us."

As the end of the line pulled away, Ethan squinted into the darkness. Now he heard it too, and it wasn't walking.

It was running.

His mouth went dry and he was suddenly aware of his heart banging madly against his chest.

"It's time to point your gun, Hecter," Ethan said.

"Something's coming?"

"Something's coming."

Maggie took a few steps back.

Ethan said, "I know you're scared, but you're our light, Maggie. No matter what you see coming down that tunnel, stand your ground. If you run, we all die. Understand?"

The splashing was getting louder, closer.

"Maggie? Do you understand me?"

"Yes," she whimpered.

Ethan pumped the shotgun.

"Hecter, is your safety off?"

"It is."

Ethan glanced back, tried to spot Theresa and Ben in the crowd, but they were too far away and the light was shit.

Ethan tugged the black synthetic stock into his shoulder and stared down the barrel. The sights were a self-luminous tritium unit that popped nicely in the dark—three soft green dots.

Ethan said, "You're shooting slugs, not buckshot."

"So there's no spread?"

"Exactly. Be accurate."

"What if I run out?"

"Cross that bridge when—"

It came out of the dark at a full sprint, barreling low on all fours at an astonishing rate of speed.

Greyhound fast.

Ethan aimed.

Hecter fired.

Muzzle flash electrifying the tunnel and wrecking Ethan's vision for a millisecond.

When Ethan could see again, the abby was still coming, twenty feet and two seconds away.

Maggie hyperventilating, "OhGodohGodohGodohGodoh—"

Ethan fired, the stock jerking back into his shoulder, the report of the shotgun in this confined space like a cannon going off.

The abby tumbled to a stop three feet from Ethan's boots, a large chunk of skull blown out of the back of its head.

Hecter said, "Wow."

His voice sounded muffled against the ringing in Ethan's ears.

They began to jog up the tunnel, chasing the end of the line, which was now just a point of firelight in the distance. As Ethan's hearing returned, he picked out new howls echoing through the tunnel.

"Faster," Ethan said.

He could hear the abbies' footfalls in the stream, closing in behind them.

Kept glancing back into the dark, kept seeing nothing.

And they were running, Maggie out in front, Ethan and Hecter abreast, elbows grazing every few strides.

They crossed a junction.

Through the tunnel to their right came screaming, shrieking, wailing—

HAROLD BALLINGER

The people at the back shouted first.

Screams in the darkness.

Human.

Inhuman.

"—Run, run, run, run, run, run—"

"—Oh God they're here—"

"—Help me—"

"—No no no noooo—"

A great surge pushing through the line, people falling in the water.

More cries for help.

Then agony.

Everything unraveling so goddamned fast.

Harold spun around to go back, but there was nothing to go back to. All the torches had been extinguished. Only darkness and screaming—an explosion of noise ricocheting off the walls of the culvert—and all he could think was that this must be what hell sounded like.

He heard gunshots in an adjacent tunnel.

Kate?

Tiffany Golden screamed his name. Shouting at him, at everyone to come on. Hurry. Don't just stand there.

She was thirty feet up the tunnel and clutching their group's last torch.

People shoved past Harold.

Someone's shoulder butted him back into the wall of crumbling concrete.

The screams of the dying were getting closer.

Harold started running, sandwiched between two women, their elbows punching into his side as they raced ahead of him toward the diminishing firelight.

He didn't think they had that much farther to go. Three, four hundred yards at the most before the tunnel opened into the woods.

If they could make it outside, even half of them—

The torch in the distance vanished with a shout.

Instantaneous dark.

The screams tripling in volume.

Harold could taste the panic in the air.

Some of it his own.

He was knocked down in the stream of water, feet trampling over his legs, then his body. Tried to get up, got knocked down again, people scrambling over him like an obstacle, someone stepping on his head.

Rolling out of the way, he climbed back onto his feet.

Something streaked past him in the dark.

It reeked of decay.

Several feet away, a man begged for help over the sound of bone and cartilage crunching.

Harold's nerve flattened under a veil of crushing disbelief.

He should go.

Just run.

The poor bastard beside him went quiet, and now there was only the sound of the monster devouring its kill.

How could this possibly be happening?

Fetid breath hit his face.

Inches away, a low growl began.

Harold said, "Don't do this."

His throat felt suddenly hot. His chest turned wet and warm. He could still breathe, and he felt no pain, but there was so much blood jetting out of his neck.

Already he felt light-headed.

Harold sank down in the freezing stream as the beast opened his stomach with a swipe.

There was only a distant, blunted pain as the abby began to eat.

All around him were the moans and cries of the dying, the scared.

People still rushed past him in the dark, fighting to get to safety.

He didn't make a sound.

Didn't fight back.

Paralyzed by shock, blood loss, trauma, fear.

He couldn't believe this was happening to him.

The thing ate him with the intensity of a creature that hadn't fed in days, its rear talons pinning him down by his legs, front talons nailing Harold's arms to the concrete.

And still no pain to speak of.

He was one of the lucky ones, he figured.

He'd be dead before the real pain hit.

ETHAN

—Pure human suffering and terror.

Chaos.

Ethan shouted, "Don't stop! Keep going!"

Thinking, *Had another group been run down in an adjacent tunnel?*

Unimaginable.

To be overtaken down here.

People climbing over one another to escape as the monsters reached them.

Torches dropped.

Extinguished in the stream.

Devoured in the dark.

Up ahead, the torchlight in Ethan's group had disappeared.

Ethan said, panting, "Where'd they go?"

"I don't know," Hecter said. "The light just vanished."

The water under Ethan's boots was rushing now and they were moving into a cold, steady breeze.

They emerged from the tunnel onto a rocky streambed, and for a moment, the sound of the abbies was replaced by the roar of white water, close but invisible in the dark.

Ethan stared up the hillside, saw the torches trailing up into a forest.

He pointed them out to Hecter and Maggie, and said, "Follow the lights."

"You're staying?" Hecter asked.

"I'll be along."

The shrieks of the abbies cut through the crush of the falls.

"Go!" Ethan said.

Hecter and Maggie headed off into the trees.

Ethan racked a fresh shell into the tube and climbed several feet up the bank to a flat perch. His eyes were slowly adjusting. He could discern the silhouettes of trees and even the cascade in the distance, the black water starlit against the sky where it arced over a ledge several hundred feet above.

Ethan's quads burned from sprinting through the tunnel, and despite the cold, his undershirt was soaked with sweat.

An abby exploded out of the tunnel and stopped in the streambed.

Took in its new surroundings.

Looked at Ethan.

Here we go.

Its head twitched to the side.

When the slug hit the abby's center mass, it fell back into the stream.

Two more abbies ripped out of the tunnel.

One rushed to its fallen comrade and let out a low, pulsing cry.

The other made a beeline for Ethan, scrabbling up the rocky bank on all fours.

Ethan racked a new shell, shot a slug through its teeth.

When it fell, the other one was right behind it, and two more were already out of the tunnel.

Ethan pumped and fired.

The other two were coming and still more screams rising up behind them.

He took the first one down with a gut shot but missed the head of its partner.

Racked another shell.

Fired at point-blank range and hit just below the neck.

Blood sprayed in Ethan's eyes.

He wiped his face as another abby joined the party.

Ethan pumped, aimed, squeezed the trigger.

Click.

Shit.

The abby heard the noise.

It lunged.

Ethan threw down the empty shotgun, drew his Desert Eagle, and put a round through its heart.

Gun smoke clouded the air, Ethan's heart hammered away, and there were screams still coming up the tunnel.

Go, go, go!

He holstered the pistol, grabbed the shotgun, and climbed away from the stream, clawing his way through rocks and dirt until he reached the trees, sweat pouring into his eyes with a salty burn.

There were lights in the distance.

Screams behind him.

He slung the shotgun over his shoulder and ran.

After a minute, the sound of the abbies changed.

They were outside now.

Many of them.

He didn't look back.

Kept going.

Kept climbing.

ADAM TOBIAS HASSLER

HASSLER EXPEDITION
NORTHWEST WYOMING
678 DAYS AGO

Brightly colored algae rims the bank, and jets of mineral water bubble where they surface up from the molten underworld below. The smell of sulfur and other minerals is strong.

Hassler strips naked in the falling snow and covers his clothes and gear under the stinking duster. Hustling through the grass, he glides into the pool and groans with pleasure.

Out in the center, it is deep and clear and sky blue.

He finds a spot near the shore a foot and a half deep and stretches out on a long, smooth rock that boasts a natural incline.

Pure, unabashed pleasure.

As if it was made for this very thing.

He reclines in the hundred-and-four-degree pool, the snow pouring down, letting his eyes close for little bursts of euphoria that remind him of what it felt like to be human. To live in a civilized world of convenience and comfort. Where the probability of death didn't shadow every moment.

But the knowledge of where he is, of who he is, of why he is here is never far. A tense voice—the one that has kept him alive for the last eight hundred and something days in the wild—whispers that it was foolish to stop for a soak in this pool. Indulgent and reckless. This isn't a spa. A swarm of abbies could appear at any time.

He's normally vigilant to a fault, but this pool is nothing short of a gift, and he knows the memory of his time here will sustain him for weeks to come. Besides, the map and compass are useless in the midst of a blizzard. He's socked in until the weather passes.

He shuts his eyes again, feels the snowflakes alighting on his lashes.

Off in the distance, he hears a sound, like water shooting out of the blowhole of a whale—one of the smaller geysers erupting.

His own smile surprises him.

He first saw this place in the faded color photos of the "XYZ" Encyclopedia Britannica volume in his parents' basement—a 1960s crowd watching from the boardwalk as Old Faithful spewed boiling mineral water.

He's dreamed of coming here since he was a boy. Just never imagined that his first visit to Yellowstone would be in conditions such as these.

Two thousand years in the future, and the world gone all to hell.

Hassler grabs a handful of gravel and begins to abrade the dirt and filth that has accumulated on his skin like body armor. In the middle of the pool, where the deep water covers his head, he submerges himself completely.

Clean for the first time in months, he climbs out of the pool and sits in the frosted grass to let his body cool.

Steam lifts off his shoulders.

He feels woozy from the heat.

Across the meadow, evergreens stand ghost-like, almost invisible through the steam and the snow.

And then—

Something he wrote off as a shrub begins to crawl.

Hassler's heart stops.

He straightens and squints.

Can't pinpoint how far away it is,

but certainly inside of a hundred yards. Easy to mistake for a man crawling on all fours at this distance, except there are no men in the world anymore. At least not beyond the electrified, razor-wired fence that surrounds the town of Wayward Pines.

Well, actually, there is one.

Him.

The figure draws closer.

No.

Figures.

Three of them.

You idiot.

He's naked, and his best means of defense—a .357—is tucked away in the pocket of his duster on the far side of the pool.

But not even his Smith & Wesson offers much comfort against three abbies at close range in snowstorm visibility. If he were prepared, if he had spotted them farther out, he might have dropped one or two with his Winchester. Put a bullet through the last one's skull point-blank with the revolver.

This line of thought is pointless.

They're coming toward the pool.

Hassler eases soundlessly back into the water, all the way up to his neck. He can scarcely see them now through the steam, prays that lack of visibility cuts both ways.

As the abbies close in, Hassler lowers himself to his eyes.

It is a mature female and two lankier adolescents, each of whom clock in around one twenty—easily lethal. He's seen smaller ones than this bring down full-grown bison.

The female is the size of them both combined.

From sixty feet away, Hassler watches as the mother stops at his pile of clothes and gear.

She lowers her nose to his duster.

The young ones come up alongside her and sniff as well.

Hassler rises a few millimeters until his nose is just above the surface.

With a long, penetrating breath, he goes under, blowing enough air out of his lungs so his body will sink.

Soon, he's sitting on the rocky floor of the pool.

Streams of burning water shoot up through tiny fissures under his legs.

He shuts his eyes, and as the pressure and the ache intensifies in his lungs, the oxygen deprivation manifests as explosions of light.

He digs his fingernails into his legs.

The thirst for breath growing exponentially.

All-consuming.

When he can't stand it anymore, he surfaces and drinks in a gulp of air.

The abbies are gone.

He turns slowly in the water—inch by inch by—

Freezes.

The urge to jerk back, to just run, is almost irresistible.

Ten feet away at the edge of the pool, one of the young abbies crouches down beside the water.

Motionless.

Head cocked slightly to one side.

Transfixed.

Studying its reflection?

Hassler has seen more than his fair share of these monsters, but mainly through his riflescope. At a distance.

He's never been this close to one undetected.

He can't take his eyes off its heart: the beating of the muscle visible through the translucent skin, the blood pumping through its arteries—purple highways converging center mass. All obscured and

104

blurred as if he watches it behind a sheet of quartz.

The abby has small eyes that remind him of black diamonds—hard and other-worldly.

But strangely enough, it isn't the monster's horrific qualities that so unnerve him.

Shining through the five-taloned claws, the rows of razor teeth, and the devastating physical strength is its humanness. These things have so clearly evolved from us, and now the world is theirs. David Pilcher, Hassler's boss and the creator of Wayward Pines, estimated there were half a billion abbies on this continent alone.

The steam is thick, but Hassler doesn't dare to slip back under the surface.

He doesn't move.

And still the abby watches its reflection in the pool.

It will either see him and he will die, or—

Off in the distance, the mother shrieks.

The young abby's head lifts.

The mother shrieks again, her voice filling with the intensity of a threat.

The abby scuttles off.

Hassler listens as the trio moves away

from the pool, and by the time he chances the smallest degree of movement—a quick turn of the head—they have vanished into the snowstorm.

Hassler waits for a break in the snow, but it never comes. He climbs out of the pool and brushes three inches of powder off his duster and dries off each foot before sliding them into the boots.

He puts the duster on wet and grabs the rest of his gear and jogs across the clearing toward the stand of pines. Ducks under a canopy of low-hanging limbs that protect the ground as thoroughly as a thatched roof. Already shivering, he drops everything and tears open his pack. The old-man's beard lies on top, and underneath it a bundle of dry tinder that he collected that morning.

The lichen takes the third spark.

As the twigs begin to crackle, Hassler breaks off several larger limbs within reach and snaps them over his knee.

The fire roars.

The cold departs.

He stands naked in the heat of the flames.

Soon, he is dressed and comfortable,

leaning back against the trunk of the tree with his hands held out to the fire.

Beyond his weather-protected nook, snow pours down into the meadow.

Night creeps in.

He is warm.

Dry.

And for the moment . . .

Not dead.

All things considered, in this shitty new world, that's about as much as a man can hope for at the end of a long, cold day.

The next time his eyes open, the sky through the branches is infused with deep blue and the meadow lies buried beneath a foot of sparkling white.

The fire burned out hours ago.

The saplings in the meadow bend under the weight of snow like little arches.

Courtesy of the hot springs, it's the first time in months that, as Hassler struggles onto his feet, he doesn't feel as stiff as a rusted hinge.

He's thirsty but his water froze overnight.

He eats just enough jerky to beat back the mad, raving hunger he always wakes to.

Lifting his rifle, he scopes the clearing for any sign of movement.

It's a good twenty or thirty degrees colder than yesterday—barely above zero—and plumes of steam ascend in a perpetual cloud off the hot springs.

Otherwise, nothing moves in that vast winterscape.

He digs out his compass and the little patch of map and then heaves his pack onto his shoulders.

Hassler crawls out from under the overhanging branches and sets out across the meadow.

It is cold and perfectly still, the sun on the rise.

In the center of the meadow, he stops and glasses the terrain through the scope of his Winchester.

For the moment at least, the world is his alone.

As the sun climbs, the glare off the snowpack becomes painful. He would stop to retrieve his sunglasses, but the welcome darkness of the forest is just within reach.

It's all lodgepole pine.

Two-hundred-foot giants with straight, thin trunks and narrow crowns.

Forest travel is considerably more dangerous, and at the edge of the trees

Hassler pulls the .357 out of an inner pocket of his duster and checks the load.

The forest climbs.

The sun pushes through the pines in splashes of light.

Hassler crests a ridge.

A lake comes into view that shines like a jewel. Close to shore, the water has frozen, but it's still liquid out in the center. He sits on a bleached tree stump and raises the butt of the rifle to his shoulder.

The lake is immense. He scopes the shoreline. There's nothing in the direction he intends to travel but unblemished, glittering white.

On the opposite side—a couple miles away—he spots a bull in a bloody patch of snow pulling long ropes of intestines out of a massive grizzly bear whose throat the abby has torn out.

Hassler starts down the gentle slope.

At the lakeshore, he studies the map again.

The forest comes close to the water, and keeping between the shore and the trees, he makes his way around to the western side of the lake.

The trek through the snow has worn him out.

Hassler unslings his rifle from his shoulder and collapses near the water's edge. In proximity, he sees that the ice isn't thick. Just a fragile crust from the hard overnight freeze. This snow has come early. Way early. By his reckoning, it's only July.

He scopes the shoreline again.

The woods at his back.

Nothing moves but that abby across the lake, its entire head now buried inside the grizzly's belly—gorging itself.

Hassler leans back against his pack and takes out the map.

There is no wind, and with the sun directly above him, he feels warm down to his bones.

He loves mornings—without a doubt, his favorite time of day. There is something hopeful about waking in the early light and not yet knowing what the day has in store. Emotionally speaking, late afternoons are the hardest, with the light beginning to fail and the knowledge setting in that he'll be spending another night outside, alone in the dark, the threat of an awful death forever in the wings.

But in this moment at least, the coming night feels very far away.

Once again his thoughts turn north.

To Wayward Pines.

To the day he'll reach its fence and return to safety.

To that little Victorian house on Sixth Street.

And to the woman he loves with a ferocity he will never fully grasp. It was for her alone that he willingly abandoned his life in 2013, volunteering to be put into suspended animation for two thousand years, with no idea of what kind of a world he'd be waking to. But just knowing it would be one with Theresa Burke alive in it, and her husband, Ethan, long since dead, was more than enough for him to risk everything.

He pairs the map with the compass.

The most prominent feature in the region is a ten-thousand-foot peak that was once called Mount Sheridan. The top thousand feet of the peak stand above the timberline—blown stark white against the purple sky. It's windy at the summit, with streamers of snow spraying off the top.

An hour's walk in prime conditions.

Two or three in a foot of newly fallen snow.

For now, it simply represents his north.

The direction of home.

THE RICHARDSONS

Bob climbed out of the car and closed the door gently after him.

The woods were quiet, the screams in town distant.

He walked a little ways out from the hood and tried to think.

Leaving town had been the right choice. They were still alive.

The dome light in the car kicked off.

Darkness closed in.

He eased down onto the pavement and put his face between his knees. Wept softly. After a minute, the car door opened behind him and the interior lights threw color on the road.

His Wayward Pines wife walked over.

"I said I needed a minute," Bob said.

"Are you crying?"

"No." He wiped his eyes.

"Oh my God, you are."

"Leave me alone please."

"Why are you crying?"

He gestured toward town. "This isn't enough?"

She sat down beside him.

"You had someone, didn't you?" she said. "Before Wayward Pines, I mean."

He made no response.

"Your wife?"

"His name—"

"His?"

"Was Paul."

They just sat there in the road.

Breathing.

Barbara finally said, "This must have been awful for you."

"I'm sure it wasn't any picnic on your end."

"You never seemed like you were really—"

"I'm sorry."

"Me too."

"How is this remotely your fault? None of this was our choice, Barbara. You were never married before, were you?"

"You were my first. In more ways than one."

"God, I'm so sorry."

"How is this remotely your fault?" Barbara laughed. "The fifty-year-old virgin—"

"And the queen."

"Sounds like a bad movie."

"Doesn't it?"

"How long were you and Paul . . . ?"

"Sixteen years. I just can't believe he's dead, you know? That he's been dead for two thousand years. I always thought I would be with him again."

"Maybe you still will."

"That's nice of you to say."

She reached over, took hold of his hand, and

said, "These last five years, you're all I've had, Bob. You always treated me with care. With respect."

"I think we made it work about as well as it possibly could."

"And we did make damn good muffins."

Somewhere out there, gunshots echoed across the valley.

"I don't want to die tonight, honey," she said.

He squeezed her hand. "I'm not going to let that happen."

BELINDA MORAN

The old woman sat in her leather recliner, the footrest extended, a dinner tray on her lap. By candlelight, she turned the cards over, halfway through a game of Solitaire.

Next door, her neighbors were being killed.

She hummed quietly to herself.

There was a jack of spades.

She placed it under the queen of hearts in the middle column.

Next a six of diamonds.

It went under the seven of spades.

Something crashed into her front door.

She kept turning the cards over.

Putting them in their right places.

Two more blows.

The door burst open.

She looked up.

The monster crawled inside, and when it saw her sitting in the chair, it growled.

"I knew you were coming," she said. "Didn't think it'd take you quite so long."

Ten of clubs. Hmm. No home for this one yet. Back to the pile.

The monster moved toward her. She stared into its small, black eyes.

"Don't you know it's not polite to just walk

into someone's house without an invitation?" she asked.

Her voice stopped it in its tracks. It tilted its head.

Blood—from one of her neighbors no doubt—dripped off its chest onto the floor.

Belinda put down the next card.

"I'm afraid this is a one-player game," she said, "and I don't have any tea to offer you."

The monster opened its mouth and screeched a noise out of its throat like the squawk of a terrible bird.

"That is *not* your inside voice," Belinda snapped.

The abby shrunk back a few steps.

Belinda laid down the last card.

"Ha!" She clapped. "I just won the game."

She gathered up the cards into a single deck, split it, then shuffled.

"I could play Solitaire all day every day," she said. "I've found in my life that sometimes the best company is your own."

A growl idled again in the monster's throat.

"You cut that right out!" she yelled. "I will not be spoken to that way in my own home."

The growl changed into something almost like a purr.

"That's better," Belinda said as she dealt a new game. "I apologize for yelling. My temper sometimes gets the best of me."

ETHAN

The light in the distance was getting closer, but he couldn't see a thing around him.

Tripping every few steps, he tore up his hands as he grasped for branches in the dark.

Wondering, *Could the abbies track us? By scent? Sound? Sight? All of the above?*

The torchlights were close.

He could see his group in the illumination.

Ethan came out of the trees at the base of the cliff.

There was already a line of people moving like ants up the rock, the glow of torches high above like a strand of Christmas lights strung across the cliff.

Ethan had climbed this route only once before while infiltrating the Wanderers, Kate and Harold's secret group.

Steel cables had been bolted into the rock in a series of harrowing switchbacks over man-made footholds and handholds.

A dozen people stood around the base of the cliff, waiting their turn to ascend. He looked for his family, but they weren't there.

Hecter walked over. "This is a bad idea," he said. "Putting children on the cables in the dark."

Ethan thought of Ben, drove his son out of his mind.

"How many are coming?" Hecter asked.

"More than we can handle."

Down the mountainside, Ethan could hear branches snapping.

He had a pocketful of twelve-gauge shells and he started feeding them into the magazine while he watched the edge of the forest.

With the last shell in the tube, he leveled the shotgun on the woods.

Thinking, *Not yet. Just a little bit longer please.*

Hecter tapped Ethan's shoulder, and said, "It's time."

They went up the rock face, clutching the freezing cable.

By the time Ethan reached the third switchback, the forest below him was alive with screams and shrieks.

Wails lifting up through the trees.

The nearest torch was twenty feet above, but the stars were numerous and bright enough to light the rock.

Ethan glanced down the cliff as the first abby came out of the trees.

Another appeared.

And another.

Then five more.

Then ten.

Soon there were thirty of them gathered at the base.

He kept climbing, trying to focus on clutching the cables and stepping sure-footedly, but every time he looked down there were more abbies than before.

The rock went vertical.

He wondered how Theresa and Ben had fared.

Were they safe in the Wanderers' cavern now?

Above him, a scream that plummeted in his direction.

Closer, closer, closer, closerclosercloser . . .

Growing exponentially louder until it was right on top of him.

He looked up as a man rocketed past, arms flailing, eyes gaping wide with horror.

He missed Ethan by two inches and his head struck a ledge twenty feet below, the blow sending him somersaulting the remaining distance toward the forest floor in dead silence.

Jesus.

Ethan's legs felt like liquid.

A tremor moved through his left foot.

He leaned into the rock and clutched a handhold. Shut his eyes. Let the panic course through him and burn itself out.

The terror passed.

Ethan went on, pulling himself up foot by foot on the rusted cable as the abbies ripped apart the man who'd lost his footing on the cliff.

Ethan reached the plank walkway.

Six inches wide, it traversed the face of the cliff.

Hecter was already halfway across.

Ethan followed.

The forest was now three hundred feet below.

Wayward Pines was somewhere out there, the town still dark but filled with distant screams.

On the rock below, Ethan spotted movement.

White forms climbing toward him.

He shouted to Hecter, "They're on the cliff!"

Hecter looked down.

The abbies climbed fast, fearlessly, like the possibility of falling did not exist.

Ethan stopped, holding the cable with one hand while he tried to get a decent grip on the Mossberg.

No use.

He called out to Hecter, "Come here!"

Hecter turned awkwardly on the narrow planks and headed back toward Ethan.

"I need you to hold my belt," Ethan said.

"Why?"

"There's not enough room up here for me to stand and aim."

"I don't understand."

"Hold the cable with one hand, grab my belt with the other. I'm going to lean out over the edge and take a clean shot."

Hecter sidestepped the last few feet to Ethan and grabbed hold of his belt.

"I assume it's buckled?" he asked.

"Good one. You got me?"

"I got you."

And still it took three seconds for Ethan to steel his nerve.

He let go of the cable and slid the strap of the shotgun off his shoulder, aimed the luminous sight down the face of the cliff.

Ten abbies were making an ascent in a tight cluster. He tried to focus, to put the fear out of his mind, but he kept seeing that man falling toward him, his head cracking open on the rock.

The scream.

The silence.

The scream.

The silence.

Ethan's stomach turned. The world seemed to rush up at him and fall away at the same time.

Get it together.

Ethan drew a bead on the leader.

The shotgun bucked him back against the cliff and the report raced across the valley, bounced off the western wall of rock, and returned.

The slug hit the lead abby.

It peeled off with a shrill screech and tumbled down the rock, crashing into four more and knocking them over like bowling pins.

The others held fast.

They had climbed to within sixty feet of the plank.

Once again Ethan leaned out over the ledge, heard Hecter groaning, and imagined the cable biting into Hecter's fingers.

The remaining abbies had taken the hint and spread out.

He took his time shooting them down from left to right.

No misses.

Watched them plunge into the darkness, taking out a handful of others who had just begun to climb.

He was out of ammo.

"All right," Ethan said.

Hecter pulled him back onto the plank and they hurried on, crossing the rock face until they rounded the corner at the end.

They rushed up the widening ledge into the mountain.

Ethan could hardly see a thing in the passage, and up ahead, the door to the cavern was shut.

He pounded the wood.

"Two more out here! Open up!"

The bolt slid back on the other side, hinges creaking as it opened.

Ethan hadn't noticed the door his first time here, but now he made a careful study. It had been constructed of pine logs stacked horizontally and cemented together with an earth-based mortar.

He followed Hecter inside.

Kate shut the door after him and shot a heavy steel rod back into its housing.

Ethan said, "My family—"

"They're here. They're safe."

He spotted them over by the stage, flashed an *I-love-you* sign.

Ethan surveyed the cavern—several thousand square feet with kerosene lamps hanging from wires in the low rock ceiling.

A scattering of furniture.

Bar on the left.

Stage on the right.

Both rickety-looking, as if they'd been assembled out of scrap wood. At the large fireplace toward the back, someone was already building a fire.

Looked to Ethan like only a hundred people or so, everyone huddled around torches, eyes twinkling in the firelight.

He said, "Where are the other groups?"

Kate shook her head.

"It's only us?"

As her eyes welled up, he held her. "We'll find Harold," Ethan said. "I promise you that."

The abby screams reverberated through the passage beyond the door.

"Where's our army?" Ethan asked.

"Right here."

He looked at a half-dozen scared-shitless people

who had no business even holding weapons.

The definition of ragtag.

Ethan examined the door again. The bolt was a long piece of solid metal, half an inch thick. It spanned the five-foot wide door, which had been expertly cut to fit snugly into the arch. The housing looked durable.

Kate said, "We could all stand right outside the door. Shoot anything that tried to come down the passage."

"I don't like it. No telling how many of those things are coming, and no offense"—Ethan glanced at the terrified faces surrounding him— "but how many of you can shoot accurately in a pressure situation? These things don't go down easy. Those of you with .357s? You'd better score head shots every time. No, I think we stay in here. Pray the door holds."

Ethan turned and addressed the rest of the group. "I need everybody to move back to the far wall. We're not out of the woods yet. Keep quiet."

Everyone began to migrate away from the stage and the bar, grouping near the sofas against the rear wall of the cavern.

Ethan said to Kate, "We're going to stay right here, in front of this door. Anything that gets through dies. Where's the bag of ammo?"

A young man who worked at the dairy said, "I've got it right here."

Ethan took it from him and dropped it on the floor. He knelt over it, and said, "I need some light please."

Maggie held the torch over his head.

He rifled through ammunition, grabbed a box of two-and-three-quarter-inch Winchester slugs for himself, and then handed out backup ammo to everyone else.

Moving twenty feet back from the pine-log door, Ethan ghost-loaded the Mossberg as an unsettling hush fell upon the cavern.

Maggie and another man stood behind the shooters with torches.

Kate stood next to Ethan with a shotgun of her own, and he could hear her struggling not to break down.

Then suddenly—movement out in the passage.

Kate drew in a sharp breath, wiped her eyes.

Ethan could feel a fight coming. He glanced back, tried to find his family amid the crowd, but they had withdrawn into the shadows. He had come to terms with the possibility of his own death. There was no coming to terms with seeing an abby tear into his only son or disembowel his wife. There would be no going forward after that. Whether he lived or not, he would not survive.

If the abbies got through that door, and there were more than ten of them, everyone in the cavern would die horrible deaths.

He'd expected a scream but instead came the

sound of talons clicking on the stone floor of the passage.

Something scraped across the logs on the other side of the door, and then it began to scratch around the metal handle.

PILCHER

The town of Wayward Pines lay in ruin—buildings turned upside down, cars scattered, roads cracked in two. Even the hospital was destroyed, the top three floors sheared off. Ethan's house in particular had seen the worst of it—crushed to pieces, the aspen trees in the backyard snapped in half and shoved through the windows.

This architectural miniature of Wayward Pines had been commissioned by David Pilcher in 2010, and he'd spared no expense for the elaborate model, whose price tag came in at $35,000. For two thousand years, it had stood under glass as the centerpiece of his office, a tribute not only to the town itself, but his own boundless ambition.

It had taken him fifteen seconds to destroy it.

Now he sat on a leather sofa, watching the wall of monitors as the real town came apart at the seams.

He'd killed power to the entire valley, but the surveillance cameras ran on batteries, and most were night vision–enabled. The screens showed what the cameras saw, and the cameras were in every room of every home. In every business. In bushes. Hidden in streetlamps. They triggered off the microchips embedded in every resident of Wayward Pines, and, my, were they popping tonight.

Almost every monitor lit up.

On one screen: an abby chasing a woman up a flight of stairs.

On another: three abbies ripping a man apart in the middle of a kitchen.

—A mob of people running for their lives down the middle of Main Street, overtaken by abbies in front of the candy store.

—An abby devouring Belinda Moran in her recliner.

—Families sprinting down hallways.

—Parents trying to shield children against a horror they were incapable of stopping.

So many frames of suffering, terror, and despair.

Pilcher took a drink from a bottle of scotch—this one from 1925—and tried to think about how to feel about this. There was precedent of course. When God's children rebelled, God laid down a righteous beating.

A soft voice, the one he'd long since learned to ignore, whispered through the gale-force madness in his head, *Do you really believe you're their God?*

Does God provide?

Check.

Does God protect?

130

Check.

Does God create?

Check.

Conclusion?

Fucking A.

The search for meaning was the cornerstone of human disquiet, and Pilcher had removed that impediment. He'd given the four hundred sixty-one souls in that valley an existence beyond their wildest fantasies. Given them life and purpose, shelter and comfort. For no other reason than he had chosen them, they were the most important members of their species since *h. sapiens* had begun to walk the savannahs of East Africa two hundred thousand years ago.

They had brought this reckoning to bear. They had demanded full knowledge, knowledge they were ill-equipped to stomach. And when faced with the truth from Ethan Burke, they had revolted against their creator.

Still, watching their deaths on the monitors wounded him.

He had treasured their lives. This project meant nothing without people.

But still—fuck them. Let the abbies have them all.

He had a couple hundred people still in suspension. This wouldn't be the first time he'd started over, and his people in the mountain would support him through it all, unquestioningly, and with pure and total devotion. They were his army of angels.

Pilcher stood, unstable on his feet. He moved over to his desk, weaving. No one else in the superstructure knew what was happening in the valley. He'd instructed Ted Upshaw to close surveillance for the night. The reveal of what he'd done would have to be finessed.

Pilcher collapsed into his chair, lifted the phone, and dialed up dear old Ted.

PAM

She reached the fence in the dead of night. The hole Ethan Burke had dug out of the back of her left thigh radiated pain all through her leg and even up into her torso. The sheriff had cut out her microchip and left her stranded on the wild side of the fence, and up until this moment, she'd been obsessed with questioning why. Now, that curiosity was replaced as she stared up at the fence and wondered, *What the hell?*

It was silent.

No electricity humming through its veins.

Stupid thing to do, but she couldn't resist. Reaching out, she grabbed hold of the thick steel cable. Barbs bit into her palm but that was it. No jolt. There was something strangely illicit, erotic even, about touching the wire.

She let go, invigorated and wet.

Limping alongside the fence, she wondered if Burke had done this. A massive swarm of abbies had raced past her two hours ago. She'd watched them running north toward Wayward Pines from forty feet up a pine tree.

Hundreds and hundreds of them.

She quickened her pace, struggling against the burn in the back of her leg.

Five minutes later, she reached it.

The gate was open.

Locked open.

She looked back in the direction of the dark woods through which she—and that swarm of abbies—had come. She stared at the open gate.

Was it possible?

Had the swarm pushed into the valley?

Pam jogged through the gate. It hurt like hell, but she didn't slow down, just grunted through the pain.

Several hundred yards later, she heard the screams. Couldn't tell if they were human or abby at this distance, only that there were many of them. She stopped running. Her leg was throbbing. She didn't have a weapon. She was injured. And in all likelihood, a swarm of abbies had somehow entered the valley.

She was torn. The part of her psyche that whispered self-preservation urged her to make a run for the superstructure. Get somewhere safe. Regroup. Let Dr. Miter patch her up. But the part that ruled every fiber of her being was afraid. Not of the abbies. Not of any horror she might encounter in a town overrun with monsters. She was afraid she would find Ethan Burke already dead, and that was unacceptable. After what he'd done to her, there was nothing in the world she wanted more than to find that man and take him slowly apart.

Piece by agonizing piece.

TED UPSHAW

The smell of booze hit him as he opened the door to the old man's office.

Pilcher sat behind his desk, and when he saw Ted, he smiled a little too wide; his face was red, eyes gone glassy.

"Come in, come in!"

He struggled onto his feet as Ted closed the door after him.

Pilcher had wrecked the place. Two of the monitors were smashed, and the architect's miniature of Wayward Pines had capsized, the glass that had once covered the model town shattered across the floor, houses and buildings crushed amid the shards.

"I woke you, didn't I?" Pilcher said.

He hadn't actually. Ted couldn't have slept tonight if someone had injected him full of tranquilizers. But he said, "It's fine."

"Let's sit together like old friends."

There was a thickness, a deliberation, behind Pilcher's words. Ted wondered how drunk he actually was.

Pilcher staggered over to the leather couches. As Ted followed him, he saw that the monitors had been turned off in here as well.

They sat on the cool leather, facing the dark monitors.

Pilcher poured two healthy glasses of scotch from an expensive-looking bottle with the word Macallan on it and handed Ted the glass.

They clinked the crystal glasses.

Drank.

It was the first alcohol Ted had sipped in more than two thousand years. When he'd been homeless and drinking himself to death in the wake of his wife's passing, old scotch like this would have been a religious experience. But he'd lost his taste for it.

"I still remember the day we met," Pilcher said. "You were standing in the soup line of that shelter. It was your eyes that called out to me. So much grief in them."

"You saved my life."

The old man looked over at him. "Do you still trust me, Ted?"

"Of course," Ted lied.

"Of course. You shut down the surveillance hub when I told you to."

"That's right."

"You didn't even ask why."

"No."

"Because you trust me."

Pilcher stared into his glass at the swirling amber liquid.

"I did something tonight, Ted."

Ted looked up at the dark screens. Felt something go ice cold in the pit of his stomach. He looked over at Pilcher as the man raised a control tablet and typed something on the touchpad.

The screens flashed to life.

As head of surveillance, Ted had spent a quarter of his life watching these people eat, sleep, laugh, cry, fuck, and sometimes—when a fête was called—die.

"I didn't do this lightly," Pilcher said.

Ted stared at the screens, his eyes locking on one in particular—a woman crouching in the shower, shoulders heaving with sobs as a fist of talons punched through the bathroom door.

He felt suddenly ill.

Pilcher watched him.

Ted looked over at his boss. Eyes welling up with tears, he said, "You have to stop this."

"It's too late."

"How so?"

"I used our abbies in captivity to draw a swarm to the fence. Then I opened the gate. Over five hundred abbies have entered the town." Ted wiped his eyes. Five hundred. He could barely comprehend such a number. Just fifty abbies would have been an unqualified disaster.

Ted fought to keep his tone in check.

"Think about how hard you worked to gather the people in that valley. Decades. Remember the excitement you felt every time we put a new recruit into suspension. Wayward Pines isn't the streets or the buildings or the suspension units. It's nothing that you built. It's those people and you're—"

"They turned their backs on me."

"This is about your goddamned vanity?"

"I have several hundred others in suspension. We'll start again."

"People are dying down there, David. Children."

"Sheriff Burke told them everything."

"You lost your temper," Ted said. "That's understandable. Now send down a team to save whomever they still can."

"It's too late."

"Not while people are alive, it isn't. We can put them all back into suspension. They won't remember—"

"What's done is done. In a day or so, the rebellion in the valley will be finished, but I'm afraid one may be coming to this mountain."

"What are you talking about?"

Pilcher sipped his drink. "You think the sheriff did this all on his own?"

Ted squeezed his hands into fists to stop the tremor that was coming.

"Burke had help from the inside, from one of my people," Pilcher said.

"How do you know?"

"Because Burke has information he couldn't possibly have gotten without the help of someone in surveillance. Someone in your group, Ted."

Pilcher let the accusation sit.

Ice cracked in his glass.

"What information are you talking about?" Ted asked.

Pilcher ignored the question, held Ted's eyes with his own. "Your group consists of you and four surveillance techs. I know your loyalty is steadfast, but what about your subordinates? Burke had the help of one of them. Any ideas who it might be?"

"Where is this coming from?"

"Ted. That is just the wrong answer."

Ted stared down into his lap at his drink. He looked up again.

He said, "I don't know who on my team would do such a thing. This is why you shut down surveillance?"

"You run the most sensitive group in the superstructure, and it's been compromised."

"What about Pam?"

"Pam?"

"It's possible the sheriff got to her."

Pilcher laughed, derisive. "Pam would set herself on fire if I asked her to. She's missing by the way. Her microchip indicates she's in town, but I haven't heard from her in hours. I will ask you one last time—which of your men?"

"Give me the night."

"I'm sorry?"

"Give me the night to find out who did this."

Pilcher leaned back and regarded him with an unreadable intensity, and said, "You want to handle this yourself, don't you?"

"I do."

"A matter of honor?"

"Something like that."

"Fair enough."

Ted stood.

Pilcher pointed at the monitors. "Only you and I know what's happening down in the valley. For now, it stays that way."

"Yes, sir."

"It's a hard night for me, Ted. I'm grateful to have a friend like you to lean on."

Ted tried to smile, but he couldn't manage it. Just said, "I'll see you in the morning." He set his scotch glass down on a table and headed for the door.

ETHAN

Everyone went silent.

So quiet Ethan could hear the fire burning in the hearth at the back of the room.

The scratching stopped.

He heard the click-click-click of those talons again.

Retreating.

It made sense. Why would the abbies believe their prey had gone behind this door? They didn't even know what a door was. That it was something that opened into another place. Most of them were probably still out on—

Something struck the door.

The room took in a collective gasp.

The bolt rattled in its housing.

Ethan straightened.

The door took another blow—twice as hard— as if two abbies had crashed into it at the same time.

He thumbed off the safety and glanced at Hecter, Kate, and the others.

"How many are out there?" Kate asked.

"No idea," Ethan whispered. "Could be thirty. Could be a hundred."

In the darkness behind them, children were beginning to cry.

Parents trying to hush them.

And the blows to the door kept coming.

Ethan walked over to the left side where the hinges attached the door to the frame. One of the rusted brass plates popped a screw.

Kate said, "Will it hold?"

"I don't know."

The next blow came—the hardest yet.

The entire top plate detached from the frame.

Still four more below it.

Ethan called Maggie over, and in the torchlight, they watched the housing for the bolt.

With the next collision, it shook but held.

Ethan went back to Kate and asked, "Is there another way out of this room?"

"No."

The barrage continued, and the more the abbies hurled themselves against the logs, the angrier they seemed to get, now shrieking and screaming after every failed attempt.

Another plate broke loose.

Then another.

The end was coming. The thought actually crossed Ethan's mind that he should go find his family now. Give them both a quick, merciful death, because once the abbies got in, their last moments of sentience would be owned by horror.

The passage outside the door went quiet.

No scraping.

No footsteps.

The cavern held its breath.

After a long moment, Ethan approached the door and put his ear to the wood.

Nothing.

He reached for the bolt.

Kate whispered, "No!"

But he slid it back as quietly as he could manage and grasped the handle.

"Maggie, bring the light."

When she was standing behind him, Ethan pulled.

The two remaining hinges creaked loudly as they bore the full weight of the door.

The firelight brightened the passage.

It still smelled of the abbies—rot and death—but it was empty.

There were people who just sat against the rock wall and wept.

There were those who trembled silently at the horror they had seen.

Those who sat expressionless, still as stone, gazing into some private abyss.

Others plugged in.

Helped tend the fire.

Repair the door.

Organize the weaponry.

Bring food and water out of storage.

Comfort the grieving.

• • •

Ethan sat with his family on a broken loveseat at the edge of the fire. The room was warming, and Hecter played something beautiful on the piano that seemed to dial back the edge, to make everyone feel just a touch more human.

In the low light, Ethan counted their number over and over.

Kept arriving at ninety-six.

This morning, there had been four hundred sixty-one souls in Wayward Pines.

He tried to tell himself that it was possible other groups had survived. That they had somehow managed to find refuge. Someplace where the abbies couldn't get at them. Barricaded themselves in houses or the theater. Fled into the woods. But in his heart, he didn't believe it. He might have managed to buy in if he hadn't peeked through that trapdoor and seen Megan Fisher in the street and all those others getting slaughtered.

No.

In the town of Wayward Pines, eighty percent of humanity had been wiped out.

Theresa said, "I keep thinking we're going to hear someone knocking on the door. Do you think there's a chance that some of them will make it up here?"

"Always a chance, right?"

Ben's head lay in Ethan's lap, the boy asleep.

"You okay?" Theresa asked.

"I suppose, considering I made a decision that sent most of this town to a violent death."

"You didn't turn off the fence and open the gate, Ethan."

"No, I just invited it to happen."

"Kate and Harold would be dead."

"Harold probably is anyway."

"You can't look at it that way—"

"I fucked up, baby."

"You gave these people their freedom."

"And I'm sure they really had a chance to savor it as the abbies were tearing their throats out."

"I know you, Ethan. No, look at me." She turned his chin toward her. "I know you. I know you only did what you believed was right."

"I wish we lived in a world where actions were measured by the intentions behind them. But the truth is, they're measured by their consequences."

"Look, I don't know what's going to happen, but I just need to tell you, I need you to know, that I feel closer to you right now—on the brink of dying—than I have in years. Maybe ever. I trust you now, Ethan. I know you love me. I'm starting to see it like I haven't before."

"I do, Theresa. So much. You are . . . *everything*." He kissed her and she leaned into him, resting her head against the side of his shoulder.

He put his arm around her.

Soon, she was asleep.

He looked around.

The collective grief was a tangible thing. It seemed to weigh down the air with a thickness like water or dense smoke.

His hands grew cold. He dug his right one into the pocket of his parka. His fingers touched the memory shard that contained the footage of David Pilcher murdering his own daughter. Grasping it delicately between his thumb and forefinger, an H-bomb of rage blossomed in his gut.

Ted had copies of this footage as well, and Ethan had told him not to do anything with it. To stand by. But that was before the abby invasion. Did Ted know what was happening in Wayward Pines?

Ethan ran another headcount.

Still ninety-six.

Such frailty.

He thought of Pilcher, sitting in the warmth and safety of his office, watching on his two hundred sixteen flatscreens as the people he had kidnapped in another lifetime were massacred.

Voices roused him.

Ethan opened his eyes.

Theresa was stirring beside him.

The quality of the light hadn't changed, but it felt much later. Like he'd been asleep for days.

Gently lifting Ben's head off his lap, he stood and rubbed his eyes.

People were up and moving around.

Near the door, voices were raised.

He saw two separate groups, with Kate standing between Hecter and another man.

Both men were yelling.

He walked over, caught Kate's eye.

She said, "We have some people who want to go outside."

A man named Ian, who owned a shoe-repair store on Main called The Cobbler's Shoppe, said, "My wife is out there. We were separated when the four groups were forming."

"And you want to do what exactly?" Ethan asked.

"I want to help her! What do you think?"

"So go."

"He also wants a gun," Kate said.

A woman who worked in the community gardens pushed past several people and glared at Ethan. "My son and my husband are out there."

Kate said, "You understand my husband is too?"

"So why are we hiding in here instead of rescuing them?"

Hecter said, "You'd be dead within ten minutes of leaving this cavern."

"That's my choice, pal," Ian said.

"You aren't taking a gun."

Ethan broke in: "Hold on just a minute. This is a conversation for everyone."

He walked into the middle of the room, and said loudly enough for everyone to hear, "Circle up! We need to talk!"

The crowd slowly converged, bleary-eyed, bedraggled.

"I know it's been a hard night," he said.

Silence.

He sensed anger and blame in the eyes that watched him.

Wondered how much of it was truly there, how much he imagined.

"I know you're all worried about those who didn't make it in here. I am too. We barely made it ourselves. And some of you may be wondering why we didn't stop and help. I can tell you right now that if we had, this would be an empty cavern, and we'd all be dead in that valley. That's hard to hear. As the man responsible for us being in this situation . . ."

Emotion reared its head.

He let the tears come, let the tremor disrupt his voice.

"From my place at the back of the line," he said, "I saw what was happening to our people above ground. I know what these aberrations are capable of. And I think we all need to start coming to terms with a hard, hard truth. There's a chance we're all that's left of Wayward Pines."

Someone yelled, "Don't say that!"

A man stepped into the circle. He was an officer of the fête, still dressed in black, still carrying his machete. Ethan had never exchanged words with him, but he knew where he lived, that he worked at the library. He was slim and fit, with a shaved head and faint stubble across his jawline. He also carried that whiff of unearned arrogance that seems to cling to those who crave authority for the sheer sake of power.

The officer said, "I tell you what you do. You get on your hands and knees and crawl back to Pilcher and beg the man's forgiveness. Tell him *you* did this. Tell him *you* brought this shitstorm down on our heads all on your very own and that we want to go back to the way things were. That none of us signed up for this."

"It's too late," Ethan said. "You all know the truth now. You can't unknow it. There's no easy way out of this."

A short, squat man—the town butcher—pushed his way into the circle.

He said, "You're telling me my wife and daughters are dead. That at least a dozen dear friends of mine are dead. So what are you saying we *do* about it? Hide in here like a bunch of cowards and write them off?"

Ethan moved toward him, his jaw tensing. "I am not saying that, Andrew. I am not saying we write anybody off."

"Then what? What are we supposed to do?

You pulled the wool away from our eyes. But for what? To lose most of our people and live like *this?* I'd rather be enslaved. I'd rather be safe and have my family."

Ethan stopped a foot away from the man. He scanned all the faces, found Theresa's. She was crying. She was sending him love. "I may have fired the opening shot," he said, "but I didn't turn off the fence, and I didn't open the gate. The man responsible for the deaths of our families and our friends, for you even being in Wayward Pines in the first place, is alive and well two miles from where we stand. And my question for you is: Are *you* going to stand for that?"

Andrew said, "He's backed by his own private army. Those are your words."

"Yeah."

"So what do you want us to do?"

"I want you to not lose hope! David Pilcher is a monster, but not everyone in the mountain is. I'm going across the valley."

"When?"

"Right now. And I'd like Kate Ballinger and two others who can shoot to come with me."

"We should take a large group," the officer said.

"Why? So we attract more attention and get more people killed? No, we need to go light and fast. Stay unseen if at all possible. And yes, it's likely we won't come back, but the alternative is to sit here in this cave and wait for the inevitable. I say we go out swinging."

Hecter said, "Even if you make it into the mountain, you actually believe you can stop this man?"

"I do believe that."

A woman stepped out of the crowd. She still wore her costume from the night before—a ball gown with a tiara she hadn't thought to take off. Her lipstick, mascara, and eyeliner streaked garishly down her face.

"I want to say something," she said. "I know a lot of you are angry at this man. At the sheriff. My husband . . ." She took a moment to collect herself. "Was in another group. We'd been married six years. It was a forced marriage, but I loved him. He was my best friend, even though we barely talked. It's amazing how well you can come to know a person through eye contact. Through subtle glances." Murmurs of agreement rippled through the crowd. She stared at Ethan. "I want you to know that I would rather Carl be dead and I would rather die today than live in that sick illusion of a town for one more hour. Like prisoners. Like slaves. I know you did what you thought was right. I don't blame you for a thing. Maybe not everyone feels this way, but I know I'm not the only one."

"Thank you," Ethan said. "Thank you for saying that."

He made a slow turn, studying the ninety-five faces watching him, feeling the true weight of their lives on his shoulders.

He said, finally, "I'm going out that door in ten minutes. Kate, you in?"

"Hell yes."

"We need two others. I know more of you may want to come, but there could still be another attack on this cavern. We want to leave you well armed and well guarded. If you think you can shoot, if you're in exceptional physical condition, and if you can control your fear, then join me over at the door."

Ethan sat on the stage between Theresa and Ben.

The boy said, "I don't want you to go back out there, Dad."

"I know, buddy. Between you and me, I'm not all that wild about it myself."

"So don't go."

"Sometimes we have to do things we don't want to."

"Why?"

"Because they're the right things."

He couldn't imagine what was going through the boy's mind. All the lies he'd been taught in school suddenly melting against the blistering heat of the truth. Ethan could remember his dad waking him from nightmares when he was Ben's age, telling him it was just a bad dream, that there were no such thing as monsters.

But in his son's world, monsters did exist.

And they were everywhere.

How did you help a boy come to terms with something like that when you could barely face it yourself?

The boy wrapped his arms around Ethan and squeezed.

"You can cry if you want," Ethan said. "There's no shame in it."

"You're not."

"Look again."

The boy looked up. "Why are you crying, Dad? Is it because you aren't coming back?"

"No, it's because I love you. So very much."

"*Are you* coming back?"

"I'm going to try my best."

"What if you don't?"

"He's coming back, Ben," Theresa said.

"No, let's be straight with him. It's very dangerous what I have to do, son. It's possible I won't make it. If something happens to me, you take care of your mother."

"I don't want anything to happen to you." Ben started to cry again.

"Ben, look at me."

"What?"

"If something happens to me, you take care of your mother. You'll be the man of the house."

"Okay."

"Promise me."

"I promise."

As Ethan kissed the top of the boy's head, he looked over at Theresa.

She was so strong.

"You'll come back," she said, "and when you do, you'll make everything about this town better."

HASSLER

The nomad had planned to spend one last night in the wild, but the moment Hassler zipped into his bivy sack at the top of the pine tree, the realization hit: sleep would never find him.

He'd been out in the wild beyond the fence for 1,308 days. He couldn't be certain, but by his estimate, Wayward Pines was just a few miles to the north, and now that the swarm of abbies had moved out of his path, he was in the clear to go home.

Every harrowing day of his expedition, at some point, his mind had wandered to this moment. Wondering, *Would he ever see it again? What would it feel like to walk back into town? Into safety and all the things he loved?*

There had been only eight nomads sent out beyond the fence in the history of Wayward Pines. Among Pilcher's inner circle, it was seen as the ultimate honor and sacrifice. To Hassler's knowledge, no nomad had ever returned from a long-term mission. Unless one of them had come back while he was away, Hassler would be the first.

He went slowly, methodically, packing his Kelty external frame backpack for the last time—the empty one-liter water bottles, his flint and steel, an empty first-aid kit, the last few scraps of moldy buffalo jerky.

Out of habit, he sealed his leather-bound journal in its plastic bag. Everything he'd experienced and encountered in his three and a half years in the wild was contained in those pages. Days of sadness. Joy. Days he was sure would be his last. All that he'd discovered. Everything seen.

His heart racing as an abby swarm, fifty thousand strong, had sprinted across what had once been called the Bonneville Salt Flats on the Great Salt Lake.

Tears running down his face as he'd watched a life-altering sunset turn the skeletal ruins of the Portland skyline from rust to bronze.

Crater Lake—empty.

Mount Shasta—decapitated.

Standing on the ruins of Fort Point and staring across the bay at all that was left of the Golden Gate Bridge—the top hundred feet of the south tower poking out of the water like the mast of a sunken ship.

All those nights he'd spent wet and cold.

Hungry and lonely.

The gray mornings he hadn't had the will to rise out of his sleeping bag and walk on.

The nights he'd sat contentedly before a fire, smoking his pipe.

What a strange, amazing life.

And now, after all of that, he was going home.

Hassler cinched down his pack and clipped in the straps and hoisted it onto his shoulders. He'd pushed himself harder than usual these last few days, and he could feel the strain in his legs and his hips, a slowly building ache that would take several days of rest to relieve. But what did it matter now? Soon, he'd be clean and in a warm, soft bed with a full stomach. No harm in toughing it out on the homestretch.

He followed the path of a stream until it branched west.

The white noise of the water dwindled away.

The woods became dark and silent.

Every step held meaning, and each one more than the last.

A few minutes shy of dawn, he stopped.

Straight ahead stood the fence.

Something was wrong. It should've been humming with its lethal voltage, but it didn't make a sound.

A single thought screamed through his mind— Theresa.

Hassler started running for the gate.

TED

Ted's residence on Level 4 was twice the size of the others, a perk of being one of the first to join David Pilcher's inner circle. For fourteen years he'd lived in this tiny space, and it exuded the messy comfort of home, with everything (sort of) in its place.

Life in the superstructure shook out in a strange rhythm of work and leisure, and it generally took people years to find the balance. Regardless of department, work shifts were onerous. Ten-hour days, six days a week. And still, things just barely got done. For Ted, as head of surveillance, there wasn't a week in recent memory when he had worked fewer than seventy hours. The challenge had come with finding what to do, beyond sleeping, with the other seventy hours of free time in the week. He wasn't an extrovert, and even though they existed for him only on surveillance monitors, Ted felt he spent every working second with the residents of Wayward Pines. So in his time off, he wanted nothing more than to be alone.

He'd tried painting.

Photography.

A bad spell of knitting.

Excessive exercise.

Until one day, eight years ago, he'd found an antique typewriter in the ark, an Underwood Touchmaster Five. He'd carried it back to his residence, along with several boxes of paper, and set up a little writer's desk in the corner of his room.

All his life, he'd felt like he harbored within him the Great American Novel.

But now that there was no America, no anything really, what would he write?

Was there even a point to the creation of books and art when humanity lived on the precipice of extinction?

He didn't know, but as he began to punch the old keys, worn so smooth the letters were barely visible, he knew he liked writing and that he loved the feel of the Underwood under his fingers.

There was no screen.

Just the lovely, tactile click-click-click of the keys, the faint smell of ink as the paper scrolled slowly out, and him alone with his thoughts.

At first, he'd toyed with a detective novel.

That had petered out.

Then his own life story, which he quickly tired of recounting.

A couple weeks in, it hit him. All day long, he stared at surveillance monitors broadcasting hundreds of private lives in all stages of desperation. He would make the residents of Wayward

Pines his subjects. Chronicle their lives before, their integrations into the town, imagine their interior thoughts and fears.

He'd started writing, and he couldn't stop.

The stories had poured out of him and the paper had accumulated beside his desk like snowfall until he had thousands upon thousands of pages detailing the lives (as he envisioned them) of the people of Wayward Pines.

He didn't know what he would do with all these stories.

Couldn't fathom that anyone would ever want to read them.

His working title was *The Secret Lives of Wayward Pines*, and he imagined the cover as a collection of all the faces of all the people who lived down in that valley. He'd have to finish the book first, and therein lay the other problem. There was no end to the book in sight. The lives carried on. New things happened. People died. New people were introduced into town. How would one publish a living book, whose stories never ended?

The answer had come, tragically, last night as Ted sat in Pilcher's office, watching on his monitors as a swarm of abbies swept through town.

The end would come all at once as the "god" of the town brought a swift and sudden conclusion.

The knock came early to Ted's door.

He was lying in bed, where he'd been all night, paralyzed with fear. With indecision.

He said, "Come in."

His oldest friend, David Pilcher, walked inside.

Ted hadn't slept, and by the looks of it, neither had Pilcher.

The old man looked tired. Ted could see the immense hangover he carried in the squint of his eyes, and he still stunk of good scotch. A five o'clock shadow was fading in on Pilcher's face, as well as sprouting up across his shaven head in fine speckles of gray.

Pilcher pulled the chair away from Ted's writing desk, dragged it in front of the bed, and took a seat.

He looked at Ted.

He said, "What do you have for me?"

"What do I have?"

"Your team. You told me you would handle it. You would find out which of them helped Sheriff Burke orchestrate this rebellion."

Ted sighed. He sat up, grabbed his thick glasses off the bedside table, and put them on. He was still wearing his stained, short-sleeved button-down and clip-on tie. Same pants. He hadn't even bothered to take off his shoes.

Last night, in Pilcher's office, Ted had been afraid.

Now, he just felt tired and angry.

So very angry.

He said, "When you said the sheriff had information he couldn't have had otherwise, did you want to tell me what you meant by that?"

Pilcher leaned back in the chair and crossed his legs.

"No, not really. I just want you, as head of the surveillance unit, to do your job."

Ted nodded.

"I didn't think you would answer me," Ted said, "but that's okay. I know what that information is. I should've told you last night, but I was too scared." Pilcher cocked his head. "I found the footage of what you and Pam did to your daughter."

For a moment, it was painfully quiet in Ted's quarters.

"Because Sheriff Burke asked you to help him?" Pilcher said.

"I sat here all night, trying to think what to do." Ted reached into his pocket, pulled out a piece of hardware that resembled a flake of mica.

"You made a copy of the footage?" Pilcher asked.

"I did."

Pilcher leveled his gaze on the floor, then back at Ted.

He said, "You know the things I've done for our project. For us to be sitting here right now, two thousand years in the future, the last of humanity. I saved—"

"There's a line, David."

"You think so?"

"You murdered your own daughter."

"She was helping an underground—"

"There is no scenario in which killing Alyssa is okay. How do you not know that?"

"I made a choice, Ted, in that previous life, that nothing, *nothing,* was more important than Wayward Pines."

"Not even your daughter."

"Not even my sweet Alyssa. You think"—tears spilled down his face—"I *wanted* that outcome?"

"I don't know what you want anymore. You murdered an entire town. Your own daughter. Years ago, your wife. Where does it end? Where's the line?"

"There is no line."

Ted ran his fingers over the memory shard in his hand. He said, "You can still come back from this."

"What are you talking about?"

"Call everyone together. Come clean. Tell them what you did to Alyssa. Tell them what you did to the people of Wayward—"

"None of them would understand, Ted. You don't."

"This isn't about them understanding. This is about you doing what's right."

"Why would I do that?"

"For your own soul, David."

"Let me tell you something. It's the story of my life, people not understanding what I was willing to do to succeed. My wife didn't get it. Alyssa didn't get it. And I'm sad, but not shocked, that you don't either. Look at what I've created. Look at what I've accomplished. If there were history books still being written, I would be listed as the most important human being who ever lived. That isn't delusion. That's just fact. I saved the human race, Ted, because there was nothing I wasn't willing to do to succeed. No one has ever understood that. Well, two people did. But Arnold Pope is dead, and Pam's missing. You know what that means?"

"No."

"It means the dirty work now falls to me."

And suddenly Pilcher was out of the chair and moving toward the bed, Ted not understanding what was happening until the short blade of the fighting knife in his boss's hand threw a wink of light.

ETHAN

In the end, Maggie and Hecter were the only volunteers Ethan felt comfortable with. No one else in the group, not even Kate, had faced down the abbies like those two. He figured most courage would wilt in the face of a charging abby. Go with known quantities.

They armed themselves.

Maggie had only shot a .22 rifle once in her life, so Ethan loaded a Mossberg 930 with buckshot for her and filled the pockets of her trench coat with extra shells. He showed her how to hold it. How to reload. Prepped her for the aggressive recoil.

He slug-loaded a Mossberg and then a .357 Smith & Wesson for Hecter.

Kate chose the Bushmaster AR-15 with a .40 caliber Glock for backup.

Standing in the passage, Ethan glanced back at the handful of people he'd armed to guard the cavern door.

"And if you don't come back?" the officer asked.

"You've got provisions here to last a few days," Kate said.

"Then what?"

"I guess you'll have to figure that out for yourselves."

Theresa and Ben stood just inside the cavern.

They'd already said their goodbyes.

Ethan held eye contact with his wife until the heavy log door swung closed and the bolt rattled home.

It was freezing.

In the distance, daylight streamed past the opening.

Ethan said, "Nobody shoots unless we have no choice. Our best-case scenario, we get down into town without firing a shot. Once we broadcast our position, it's probably all over for us."

Kate led the way toward the light at the end of the passage.

Ethan replayed his last glimpse of Theresa and Ben as the door had shut between them.

Thinking, *Was that the last time I'll ever see you?*

Do you know how much I love you?

They stood at the end of the ledge, looking out across the valley.

It was morning.

Not a sound rising out of the town a thousand feet below.

The sunlight felt good on Ethan's face.

Maggie whispered, "It just feels like a nice, normal morning, doesn't it?"

They were too far away to see anything distinct in the streets below. Ethan pictured the pair of binoculars sitting in the bottom drawer of his desk at the station. Would've been nice to have.

He stepped to the edge and looked straight down three hundred feet of vertical stone that glistened in the sunlight.

They worked their way across the plank and rested on the other side at the top of the highest switchback.

The stone was warm in the sun.

They down-climbed.

Clutching cables.

Following the steps that had been cut into the rock.

There were no birds out.

Not even a whisper of wind.

Just the four of them, breathing quickly.

Below the tops of the trees, below the reach of the sun, the steel cables were like ice.

Then they were off the rock, standing on the soft floor of the forest.

Ethan said, "You know the way into town, Kate?"

"I think so. It's weird. I've never been here in the daylight."

She led them into the pines.

There were still patches of snow in places, footprints from the night before. They followed the tracks down the mountainside, Ethan scanning the trees, but nothing moved. The woods felt absolutely dead.

After awhile, he heard the waterfall.

They descended a steep pitch of hillside.

Reached the stream and the opening of the drainage tunnel. The abbies Ethan had shot last night lay dead in the water and on the bank.

There was mist in his face.

He stared up at a single cascade that spilled over a ledge two hundred feet above. The sunlight made a rainbow where it passed through the falling water.

"Take the tunnel into town?" Kate asked.

"No," Ethan said. "We should leave ourselves plenty of room to run."

After a quarter of a mile, the terrain leveled out and they emerged from the woods behind an old, decrepit house on the eastern edge of town, the same house, Ethan realized, where he'd found the mutilated corpse of Agent Evans when he'd first arrived in Wayward Pines.

They stopped in the weeds on the side of the house.

Up until this moment, Ethan had found comfort in the silence. Now it was disquieting. Like the world was holding its breath for something.

He said, "I was thinking on the hike down. If we could find a functional car, we could haul ass to the south end of town and not have to worry about an ambush the whole time. Kate, does that old beater in front of your house run?"

"Haven't cranked it in years. I wouldn't want to chance it."

"The car in front of mine does," Maggie said.

Ethan asked, "When's the last time you took it for a spin?"

"Two weeks ago. I got a phone call one morning, someone telling me to drive around town for a few hours."

"I've always wondered why they did that," Hecter said.

"Because roads are never completely empty in normal towns," Ethan said. "Just another ploy to make Wayward Pines feel real. Where's your place, Maggie?"

"Eighth Street, between Sixth and Seventh Avenues."

"That's only six blocks away. Where are the keys?"

"Bedside table drawer."

"You're sure."

"Hundred percent."

Ethan peeked around the corner of the house, saw bodies in the distance in the street, but no abbies.

"Let's sit for a minute," he said. "Catch our breath."

They all sat against the rotting boards of the house.

Ethan said, "Maggie, Hecter, no military experience, right?"

Headshakes.

"I was a Black Hawk pilot. Saw some insane combat in Fallujah. We have six blocks to cover across very hostile territory, and there's a right way to move in these situations to minimize exposure. From our current position, we can only see the surrounding block, but when we get across the street, our perspective will change. We'll have new information. Even though we have six blocks to contend with, we're going to look at that distance incrementally. Maggie and I will cross the street first and secure a position. I'll evaluate the area from our new vantage point, and when I give the sign, Kate and Hecter will join us. Make sense?"

Nods.

"I want to say one last thing about how we're going to move. It's called a tactical column. We'll keep close together as we run, but the pace should be controlled enough for you to stay alert. If the coast is clear, the temptation will be to focus on areas in the distance to see what's coming, but that's a mistake. If we see abbies coming from a hundred, two hundred yards out, there's time for us to react. Worst thing that can happen is a surprise ambush. One of these things coming out of a bush, around a corner, and then you don't even have time to raise your weapon. So watch your danger areas. That's top priority. If you pass a bush and you can't see what's behind it, you cover that bush. Got it?"

Maggie's shotgun had begun to tremble in her grasp.

Ethan touched her hand. "You're going to do fine," he said.

She turned away suddenly and threw up in the grass.

Kate patted her back, and whispered, "It's okay, honey. It's okay to be scared. It's right to be scared. It'll make you sharp."

Ethan considered how utterly unprepared this woman was. Maggie had never been exposed to anything approaching this level of horror and pressure and yet she was slugging her way through it.

Maggie wiped her mouth and took a few deep breaths.

"You okay?" Ethan asked.

"I can't do it. I thought I could but—"

"I know you can."

"No, I should just go back."

"We need you, Maggie. The people in the cavern need you."

She nodded.

"You'll be with me," Ethan said, "and we'll take it one step at a time."

"Okay."

"You can do this."

"I just need a moment."

He'd seen this in war. Combat paralysis. When

174

the total horror of the violence and the constant threat of death overwhelmed a soldier. In his time in Iraq, the nightmare scenario was a sniper's bullet or an IED. But even on the worst days in the streets of Fallujah, there wasn't anything that wanted to eat you alive.

He gave Maggie a hand up.

"You ready?" he asked.

"I think so."

He pointed across the street. "We're going to cross to that house on the corner. Don't think about anything else."

"Okay."

"You're going to see some bodies in the street. Just want to warn you. Ignore them. Don't even look at them."

"Danger areas." She tried to smile.

"You got it. Now stay close."

Ethan picked up his shotgun.

Butterflies in his stomach.

That old, familiar fear.

Five steps out from the side of the house, the bodies in the street were in full view. And you couldn't *not* look at them. He counted seven people, two of them children, literally ripped apart.

Maggie was keeping up.

He could hear her footsteps a few feet behind his.

They hit the street, nothing but the sound of their footfalls on the pavement.

Their panting.

Up and down First Avenue—nothing.

It was so quiet.

They crossed into the yard and accelerated the last few steps to the two-story Victorian.

Crouched down under a window.

Ethan glanced around the corner.

Made another scan up and down First.

All clear.

He looked back at Kate and Hecter and raised his right arm.

They came to their feet and started jogging, Kate out in front and moving with confidence, like she knew what she was doing, Hecter a few uncomfortable paces back. Ethan could tell the moment they saw the bodies. Hecter's face fell and Kate's jaw set and they couldn't tear their eyes away.

Ethan looked at Maggie, and said, "You did great."

Then all four of them were together again.

Ethan said, "Street's empty. I don't know why it's so quiet, but let's take advantage. All four of us this time. We'll head out into the street and go right down the middle of it."

"Why?" Hecter asked. "Isn't it safer to stay near the houses, not so out in the open?"

"Corners are not our friends," Ethan said.

He gave Hecter and Kate a minute to catch their breath.

Then he stood.

"What's the next destination?" Kate asked.

"There's a green Victorian two blocks down on the other side of the street. A row of juniper shrubs along the front. We'll get behind those. Everyone ready?"

"Want me last in line?" Kate asked.

"Yes. Cover everything on our right and glance back every so often to make sure we aren't getting flanked."

It was a deceptively peaceful morning on Eighth Street.

They jogged down the middle of the road, quaint Victorians on either side and all those white picket fences bright and perfect in the early sun. Ethan's stomach ached with hunger. He couldn't remember the last time he'd eaten.

He switched between studying the houses on their left and the road ahead.

The side yards unnerved him more than anything. Those narrow canyons between houses that led into backyards he couldn't see.

They reached the first intersection.

So strange. He'd expected the town to be thick with abbies. Wondered if they'd left. Raided town for a night and gone back out into the wild the way they'd come—through Pilcher's gate. That would simplify things if he could get control of the fence and just shut them back out.

The green Victorian was close now, two houses down.

He picked up the pace and veered toward the front yard.

Suddenly Kate was running beside him.

"What's wrong?" he asked, breathless.

"Faster," she gasped. "Just run."

Ethan jumped the curb, sprinted through the grass.

Glanced back—nothing.

They reached the junipers.

Scrambled through the branches.

Ducked down in the shadow between the bushes and the house.

Everybody out of breath.

Ethan said, "Kate, what happened?"

"I saw one."

"Where?"

"Inside one of the houses on the street."

"Inside?"

"It was just standing at a window, looking out."

"You think it saw us?"

"I don't know."

Ethan rose up slowly on his knees, peeked through the branches.

"Get down!" Kate whispered.

"I have to check. Which house was it?"

"Brown one with yellow trim. Swing on the front porch. Two gnomes in the yard."

He saw it.

Saw the screen door swinging closed, heard the distant slap of the wood smacking the frame.

But he didn't see the abby.

Ethan lowered himself back behind the bushes.

"It's outside," he said. "The screen door just closed. I don't know where it is."

"It could be coming around the house," Kate said. "Sneaking up along the side. How smart are these things?"

"Scary."

"Do you know how they hunt? How finely tuned their senses are?"

"No idea."

Maggie said, "I hear something."

Everyone hushed.

It was a clicking, scraping sound.

Ethan straightened just enough to peek through the branches again.

The abby was moving upright on the sidewalk toward the house.

The clicking was its talons on the concrete.

A large bull.

Two hundred fifty pounds at least.

It had fed recently. Ethan could barely see the pulsing of its massive heart through the dried blood and viscera that clung to its chest like a bib.

At the foot of the porch, it stopped.

Turned its head.

Ethan ducked.

Held his finger to his lips and leaned over so he could whisper in Kate's ear.

"It's at the porch, twenty feet away. We may have to engage."

She nodded.

He got onto his knees, raised the shotgun, and poked his head above the juniper.

Did you rack a shell into the tube?

Of course I racked a shell into the tube. I ghost-loaded this gun last night.

The abby was gone, but the smell of it was potent.

Close.

It shot up screaming on the other side of the bush, teeth bared, eyes like wet, black stones.

The blast was deafening, and despite the size of the thing, the slug punched it back into the grass. It went down on its back with a sucking chest wound, dark blood bubbling out like a geyser across the translucent skin.

Kate was already on her feet.

Hecter and Maggie frozen behind the bush.

Ethan said, "We have to move."

He clawed his way out.

The abby was still alive, moaning and trying to plug the quarter-size hole, watching in disbelief as it bled out.

It reached for Ethan as he moved past, a talon

catching on the hem of his jeans, tearing easily through the denim.

Kate was right behind him, Hecter and Maggie slower in coming.

"Move!" he yelled.

They ran into the street.

Sweat beaded on Ethan's forehead, streaming down into his eyes with a saltwater sting.

They crossed the next intersection.

Nothing was coming.

Ethan looked back over his shoulder down Eighth.

Maggie and Hecter were running their hearts out, arms pumping, and nothing behind them as far as he could see.

The school took up the entire next block on Ethan's right.

Playground equipment standing lonely behind a chain-link fence.

Seesaws. Swing sets. Slides. Merry-go-rounds.

A tetherball pole.

A basketball hoop.

The red brick of the school beyond.

Maggie said, "Oh my God."

Ethan looked back.

She had stopped in the middle of the street and was staring at the school.

He ran back to her.

"We have to keep going."

She pointed.

A door in the side of the building swung open and a man was standing in the threshold waving one arm.

Maggie said, "What *do* we do?"

What do we do?

One of those decisions that could decide everything.

Ethan scaled the four-foot fence and raced across the schoolyard, passing a sandbox and monkey bars in the shadow of a giant cottonwood whose yellow leaves had plastered the pavement.

The man holding open the door was Spitz, the Wayward Pines postman, an inventive position for a town that had zero need for the mail. Yet still, he'd walked the streets several days a week, stuffing mailboxes with fake junk mail, bullshit tax notices, and the like. He was a brawny, extravagantly bearded man, larger through the waist than one might think for someone who lived on his feet. Presently, he stood in a shredded black T-shirt and kilt—his fête costume—with his left arm wrapped in a piece of bloody fabric. He wore a nasty slice across his cheek and a piece of flesh had been gouged out of his right leg.

He said, "Hi, Sheriff," as Ethan arrived. "Didn't expect to see you."

"Back at you, Spitz. You look like shit."

"Just a flesh wound." The man grinned. "We thought the other groups were wiped out."

"Ours made it through the tunnels, up to the cavern."

"How many of you?"

"Ninety-six."

"I got eighty-three down in the basement of the school."

Kate asked, "Harold?"

Spitz shook his head. "I'm sorry."

Hecter said, "We thought everyone else had been killed."

"We were attacked on the way to the tunnels. Lost about thirty down by the river. Brutal. As you can see, I got in a little scuffle with one of those sons of bitches. Took five men to drag it off and if one of them hadn't had a machete it would've killed us all. I heard the gunshot a minute ago. It's what drew me outside."

"One came after us a little ways up the block," Ethan said. "We thought maybe they'd all gone back into the woods."

"Oh no. Town's still crawling with them. I've been making house raids within sprinting distance. There's people still hiding in their homes. I rescued Gracie and Jessica Turner just before dawn. Jim had nailed them into a closet. He isn't with your group, is he?"

"I saw him last night," Ethan said. "He didn't make it."

"That's too bad."

"How are your people?" Maggie asked.

183

"Three died from their wounds overnight. Two are in pretty rough shape. Probably won't last the day. A bunch of us are scraped all to hell. Everyone's freaked out. No food, just a little water from the fountains. We had a teacher in our group and if he hadn't said to come here, we'd all be dead. No question in my mind. It was war last night."

"How secure is the basement?" Ethan asked.

"Could be worse. We're locked in behind two doors in a music classroom. No windows. Only one way in and out. We've built barricades. I'm not saying it's impenetrable, but we're hanging in."

A scream erupted several blocks away.

"Better get your asses inside," Spitz said. "Sounds like whatever you killed had a buddy."

Ethan looked at Kate, back at Spitz.

"I'm headed for the mountain," he said. "For Pilcher."

Maggie said, "If there are injured people, I may be able to help. I was in school to become a nurse back in my old life."

"We'd love to have you," Spitz said.

A second scream answered the first.

Ethan said, "Do you guys have any weapons?"

"One machete."

Shit. He'd have to leave them with someone who could shoot. This group of people needed some form of protection beyond a big knife.

"Kate, you stay with them too," he said.

"You need me."

"Yes, but if we both go and get killed, then what? At least this way, you're the backup plan if I don't make it back. And meanwhile, you can protect these people."

Hecter said, like he hadn't quite fully committed to the idea, "Well, Ethan, I guess it's just you and me then."

"Will I be seeing you again, Sheriff?" Spitz asked.

"Here's hoping." Ethan grabbed Maggie's hand, and said, "Bedside table drawer?"

"Yeah, go upstairs, turn right when you come off the staircase, it's the door at the end of the hall."

"Your house locked?"

"No."

"Which one is it?"

"Pink with white trim. Wreath on the front door."

Maggie and Spitz headed into the school.

Ethan started to turn away but Kate grabbed him, her hands cold on the back of his neck. She pulled him toward her and kept pulling until their lips touched, and then she was kissing him and he was letting it happen.

She said, "Be careful," and disappeared through the door.

Ethan looked at Hecter.

The abbies were howling.

"Two blocks," Ethan said. "We can make it."

They ran through the schoolyard, between picnic tables, into an open playing field, heading straight for the fence.

Ethan glanced back, saw movement in the street behind them—pale forms on all fours.

With the shotgun slung across his shoulder, he put two hands on the fence and leapt over the top, hit the ground running on the other side.

Streaked into an intersection.

Right—clear.

Left—four abbies en route, still several blocks away.

Halfway down the block, an abby broke through the glass of a front window and charged Ethan.

"Keep running!" he screamed at Hecter, then stopped, squared up, and racked a fresh shell.

Hecter blitzed by and Ethan put the monster down with a head shot.

He chased after Hecter, and as they reached the last intersection before Maggie's house, it occurred to him that he never asked what her car looked like. There were loads of them on this block, and two parked on the curb in front of Maggie's place.

Abbies appeared straight ahead, coming toward them from Main Street, one block away, and Ethan looked back just in time to see a half dozen round the corner two blocks back near the school.

He and Hecter covered the last thirty feet through Maggie's yard.

Up the steps, onto the covered porch.

Jerked open the screen door.

Abbies screaming.

Converging.

Hecter beginning to lose his grip.

Ethan turned the doorknob, put his shoulder into the door, and rushed inside.

"Lock the door!" Ethan yelled as Hecter stumbled inside. "Stand halfway up the staircase and shoot the shit out of anything that gets in."

"Where are you going?"

"Car keys."

Ethan doubled up the stairs.

Screams audible through the walls.

At the top he turned right and raced toward the closed door at the end of the hall.

Smashed through without slowing.

Yellow walls, white crown molding.

Soft curtains, drawn.

A terrycloth robe draped over the back of a chair.

A big, pillowy bed, neatly made.

Stack of Jane Austen novels and an incense burner on the bedside table.

The cold air still redolent of fragrant smoke.

Maggie's haven.

Ethan hurried to the bedside table, pulled open the drawer.

Downstairs, the sound of glass breaking.

Wood splintering.

Snarling.

Hecter yelled something as Ethan shoved his arm toward the back of the drawer, felt his fingers graze the keys.

A shotgun blast followed.

Abbies screaming.

Hecter shouting, "Oh God!"

Shuck-shuck as he racked another slug.

Boom.

Shuck-shuck.

The spent shell falling down the stairs.

Ethan jammed Maggie's keys into the front pocket of his jeans and started down the hallway.

Hecter screamed.

No more shots.

The smooth soles of Ethan's boots slid across the hardwood floor as he reached the top of the stairs and tried to arrest his forward momentum.

Blood.

Everywhere.

Three abbies on Hecter, one tearing at his right leg, another ripping the biceps out of his arm, a third chewing its way through the fascia into his stomach.

Hecter shrieking, pounding his free hand into the skull of the abby who was gutting him.

Ethan raised the shotgun.

The first slug decapitated the abby burrowing into Hecter's stomach, and he shot the second one as it looked up snarling, but the third had a head start and it was airborne, talons out, seconds from crashing into Ethan by the time he got the Mossberg pumped and fired.

It tumbled back down the staircase and crashed into two abbies that had just torn through the front door.

Ethan racked a shell and steadied himself at the top of the staircase, trying to process his next move, fighting panic, the inescapable thought that it was all coming off the rails right now. His left arm was so tender from the Mossberg's recoil it was agony just pulling the stock snug against his shoulder.

The two abbies crawled out from under the dead abby and started for him, and Ethan shot them both down as they climbed.

The house was hazy with gun smoke and for a moment the only sound was the pneumatic hiss as the femoral artery in Hecter's leg jetted arcs of red at the front door.

The stairs looked treacherous, soaked in blood.

Hecter was groaning and shaking as he held his intestines in his hands in some kind of horrified wonder.

He was bleeding out mercifully fast, shock-white, with a cold sweat matting down his hair, giving his face a corpse-like sheen that foretold what was coming.

He stared up at Ethan with a look only a dying soldier can give the one the bullet missed.

Fear.

Disbelief.

Please-God-tell-me-this-isn't-happening.

The front door had been torn off its hinges, and through the opening, Ethan watched more abbies stream into the yard.

They would eat Hecter while he took his last breaths.

Ethan pulled his pistol, clicked off the safety.

No idea if it were true, but he said, "You're going someplace better."

Hecter just stared.

I should've let you go find the keys.

Ethan shot the pianist between his eyes. As the monsters flooded in through the front door, he was already running down the hall away from Maggie's bedroom.

He took the second doorway on his right.

Quietly shut it after him and flicked a lock that didn't stand a chance of stopping anything.

There was a claw-foot tub under a window of frosted glass.

As he moved toward it, he could hear the abbies through the door.

Eating.

Ethan set the shotgun on the pedestal sink, stepped into the bathtub.

He flipped the hasp on the window.

Raised it two feet off the sill.

Tight squeeze.

He climbed up onto the lip of the bathtub and looked out the window into a small backyard, fenced and empty.

The staircase creaked, the abbies coming.

Out in the hall, there was a great collision, like something had crashed at full speed into one of the doors.

Ethan stepped back down into the bathroom and grabbed the shotgun.

An abby screamed on the other side of the door.

Something slammed into the bathroom door.

The wood started to split down the middle.

Ethan racked a shell and shot a slug through the center of the door, heard something thunk into the wall on the other side.

There was now a slug-size hole in the door, and a puddle of blood leaking underneath it, beginning to spread across the checkered tile.

Ethan climbed up onto the rim of the bathtub.

He dropped the shotgun on the roof and squeezed through the window as another abby smashed into the door behind him.

Kneeling under the window frame, Ethan fed

191

eight shells into the tube and then draped the strap over his shoulder.

The abby was still trying to beat down the bathroom door.

Ethan closed the window and sidestepped carefully down to the edge of the roof.

It dropped twelve feet to the backyard.

He got down on his hands and knees and lowered himself over the edge, clutching the gutter until he'd managed to extend himself fully and reduce the drop to five feet.

He hit the ground hard and let his legs buckle to absorb the impact, rolled, and quickly regained his feet.

Through the panes of glass in the back door, he could see things running inside the house.

Ethan jogged around the brick patio, his muscles, his bones, every square inch of real estate on his body caught in a trajectory of increasing agony.

The fence was built of weathered one-by-sixes, five feet high, with a gate that led out into the side yard.

He peered over the top—no abbies that he could see.

Threw the latch and tugged the gate open just enough to slide through.

Up on the second floor, he heard glass explode.

He jogged alongside the house and slowed as he reached the front yard.

For the moment—empty.

He stared at the two cars parked along the curb in front of Maggie's house.

An old CJ-5 Jeep with a soft top.

A white Buick station wagon that looked prehistoric.

He dug the keys out of his pocket.

Three on the ring.

All blank.

Somewhere above him, he heard a scrape that might have been talons dragging across the tin roof.

He sprinted out into the yard.

Halfway to the curb, he looked back just in time to see an abby leap down off the roof over the porch.

It hit the ground and charged.

Ethan stopped at the sidewalk, spun, raised the shotgun, and fired a slug through its sternum.

Inside the house, screams rose up.

The station wagon was the closest.

Fifty-fifty chance of being Maggie's car.

Ethan pulled open the passenger-side door, dove in, and shut it behind him.

Climbing in behind the steering wheel, he jammed the first key into the ignition.

Nothing.

"Come on."

Key number two.

It slid in nicely.

But it wouldn't turn.

An abby exploded out the front door of Maggie's house.

Number three.

Four abbies appeared behind the first—as two of them rushed out onto the grass to their dying friend, the last of the three keys failed to even enter the keyhole.

Fuck. Fuck. Fuck. Fuck. Fuck.

Ethan ducked down in the seat and crammed himself against the floorboard.

He couldn't see a thing, but he could hear the abbies in the yard.

They're going to look in and see you and then what? Go right now.

Reaching up, he grasped the door handle and quietly tugged.

The door creaked open.

He slithered out onto the pavement, staying low against the car, hidden from the view of the house.

No abbies in the street.

He rose up until he could just see through the windows.

Counted six of them in the front yard, and through the open door he could see two more eating what was left of Hecter.

The Jeep was parked a few feet up from the station wagon's bumper.

He grabbed the shotgun out of the front seat and crawled across the pavement.

Risking visibility for several seconds, he passed between the Buick and the Jeep, but they didn't see him.

Ethan stood, stared through the plastic windows of the soft-top.

Some of the abbies had gone back inside.

One was still crouched over the carcass of the abby Ethan had just shot, whimpering.

The driver-side door was unlocked.

Ethan climbed in, set the shotgun between the seats.

He got the first key in as an abby screamed.

They'd seen him.

They were moving his way.

He turned the key.

Nope.

Started fumbling for the second key and then realized there wasn't time. He grabbed the shotgun and jumped down out of the Jeep, ran into the middle of the road.

Five were already running at him.

No misses or you die.

He shot the one out in front, and then the two to the left, backpedaling in the street as the last pair closed in.

It took three rounds to bring down the fourth.

Only one to drop the fifth as it drew within ten feet.

Three more abbies ran out of the house. In his peripheral vision, he noted movement in the streets all around him—swarms of abbies coming from every direction.

A growl behind him turned his head.

Two abbies darting straight at him on all fours like a pair of missiles—a large female and a smaller abby that couldn't have weighed more than seventy-five pounds.

He aimed at the smaller one.

Bull's-eye.

It went rolling across the pavement.

Its creamy-eyed mother skidded to a stop and crouched over her fallen young.

Let out a long, tragic howl.

Ethan ejected the spent shell.

Aimed.

The mother looked at him and there was no mistaking the intelligent, burning hate that narrowed her eyes.

She came up on her hind legs, ran at him.

Screeching.

Click.

Empty.

He dropped the shotgun and drew his pistol as he backed toward the Jeep, brought the mother down with two .50 cal rounds through her throat.

They were everywhere.

He made his move toward the Jeep.

A seven-foot-tall abby leapt onto the hood.

Ethan accidently put another two rounds—

double tap muscle memory—through its upper torso.

He reached the driver-side door as an abby appeared around the back of the Jeep.

Ethan dropped it with a head shot at point-blank range, a half second before the abby got a talon through his windpipe.

He climbed in.

Couldn't remember which key he'd tried last time and just shoved in the first one he could get between his fingers.

An abby appeared behind the plastic window on the passenger side.

A talon sliced through and a long, muscled arm reached inside.

Ethan lifted the Desert Eagle from his lap and shot it in the face as it tried to climb into the Jeep.

The key wouldn't turn.

As he fumbled with the next one, a terrifying thought crossed his mind—what if Maggie's car was actually parked across the street? Or up the curb a little ways? It's not like she ever had to drive it.

Then I will be eaten alive in this Jeep.

A slashing behind Ethan.

He glanced back as a black talon tore through the plastic rear window.

The view through the old, dirty plastic was blurry, but he could see enough of the monster to draw a bead.

He shot through the window.

Blood spattered across the plastic and the pistol's slide locked back.

Empty.

With only one magazine, it would take him a minimum of thirty seconds to dig out the box of .50 cal rounds, reload it—

Wait.

No.

He hadn't brought extra ammo for the Desert Eagle.

Only the Mossberg.

The abbies were closing in. He could see a dozen of them through the windshield and hear more heading toward him from Maggie's house.

He grasped the second key, thinking, *How strange that whether I live or die comes down to whether or not this key will turn.*

It went into the ignition.

He jammed his foot down hard into the clutch.

Please.

The engine turned over several times—

And sputtered to life.

The gurgling noise of it *was* life.

Ethan popped the emergency brake and wobbled the gearshift, which operated a three-speed manual transmission.

He shifted into reverse, then gunned the gas.

The Jeep lurched back and crashed into the station wagon, pinning a screaming abby to the bumper. Ethan shifted into first, cranked the wheel, floored the pedal.

Out into the street.

Abbies everywhere.

If he'd been driving something substantial he wouldn't have hesitated to plow right through them, but the Jeep was compact, with a narrow wheelbase that made it prone to rolling over.

He doubted it could sustain a head-on collision with even a modest-size bull.

It felt so good to accelerate.

He took a sudden left turn to miss an abby, the Jeep leaning over on two wheels.

Brought it back down, four coming straight at him, undaunted, no signs of deviating from their kamikaze course.

He turned hard, drove over the curb, plowed through a picket fence at thirty miles per hour, through the front yard of a corner lot, and punched through the fence again on the other side, the Jeep taking a thunderous jarring as it came back off the curve and hit the road, tires squealing as he straightened out the steering wheel.

The road ahead was clear.

Rpm maxed.

Ethan shifted into second.

Whatever was under the hood of this thing had some meat on its bones.

Ethan glanced in the side mirror.

A swarm of abbies, thirty or forty strong, was chasing him down the middle of the street, their screeches audible even over the roar of the eight-cylinder engine.

He hit sixty blasting through the next block.

Passed a toddler park where a dozen baby abbies were feeding on a pile of bodies in the grass.

Must have been forty or fifty bodies. One of the doomed groups.

Sixth Avenue was coming to an abrupt end.

The forest of towering pines looming in the distance.

Ethan dropped a gear.

He'd outrun the abbies by a quarter mile at least.

At Thirteenth Street, he took a hard right turn and punched the pedal again.

He drove alongside the woods for a block, and then past the hospital.

Ethan dropped one more gear, took a slow left turn onto the main drag out of town.

Floored it.

Wayward Pines dwindled away in the rearview mirror.

He drove past the goodbye sign, wondering if anyone had made it this far into the woods when the mayhem had ensued.

As if in answer to his question, he passed an Oldsmobile parked on the side of the road. Nearly every shard of glass had been busted out, the exterior covered in dents and scratches. Someone had tried to flee to the outskirts of town, only to have a group of abbies find them.

At the *Sharp Curve Ahead* sign, he veered off the road into the forest.

Kept his speed up in the trees.

The boulders appeared in the distance.

He had a pocketful of shotgun shells and no shotgun.

A devastating pistol with no rounds left.

Not exactly the ideal setup for what he was about to do.

The large outcropping that masked the entrance to the superstructure loomed a hundred yards ahead.

Ethan shifted into second, tightened his grip on the steering wheel.

Fifty yards.

He had the pedal down against the floor-board, the heat of the overworked engine coming through the vents.

At twenty-five yards, he braced himself.

The speedometer holding steady.

He was driving at forty miles per hour into a wall of rock.

THERESA BURKE

She was in Seattle, their old home in Queen Anne—her family in the backyard on one of those perfect summer evenings when you could see everything. Rainier. The Puget Sound and the Olympics across the water. Lake Union and the skyline. Everything cool and green and the water shimmering as the sun fell. All that suffering through the chill, gray days of endless drizzle was rewarded with nights like this. The city almost too beautiful to take.

Ethan stood by the grill, cooking salmon filets on planks of wine-soaked cedar. Ben strummed an acoustic guitar in a hammock. She was *there*. Everything so vibrant, the dream verging toward lucidity. She even questioned the reality as she moved to her husband and placed her hands on his shoulders, but she could smell the fish cooking, could actually *feel* the sunlight hit her eyes, and the good bourbon she was drinking was a pleasant lethargy in her legs.

She said, "I think those look ready," and then the world began to shake and even though her eyes were already open, she somehow opened them again to find Ben shaking her awake.

She sat up from the cold rock floor of the cavern, her bearings lost. For a moment, she had no idea where she was. People were running past her toward a heavy log door that now stood wide open.

The dream was fading fast, the real world rushing back in like a pounding hangover. She couldn't remember the last time she'd dreamed of her life before, and the timing now seemed especially cruel.

She looked at Ben and said, "Why is the door open?"

"We have to leave, Mom."

"Why?"

"The abbies are coming back. One of the watchers saw a swarm of them scaling the cliffs."

That jerked her back into full consciousness.

"How many?" she asked.

"I don't know."

"Why's everyone leaving the cavern?"

"They don't think the doors can handle another attack. Come on." He took hold of her hands and pulled her up onto her feet.

They moved toward the open door, panic intensifying in the cavern, people bunching closer as they neared the exit, elbows jabbing into ribs, skin brushing hard against skin. Theresa reached down and grabbed Ben's hand, pulling him in front of her.

They pushed their way through the threshold of the massive door.

The tunnel echoed with voices, everyone

fighting to reach the daylight at the opening.

Theresa and Ben emerged under a midday sky so blue it looked fake. She stepped right to the edge of the cliff and took a stomach-swimming glance straight down.

Said, "Oh Jesus."

At least twenty abbies had begun to scale the cliff.

Another fifty were gathering at the base, three hundred feet below.

More still coming out of the forest.

Ben moved toward the edge, but she held him back. "Don't even think about it."

What had started as chaos inside the cavern was escalating toward hysteria out in the open. People had seen what was coming. Some had fled back into the tunnel. Others were trying to climb higher up the mountain. A few had become frozen with fear, sitting down against the rock, trying to tune the world right out.

Those whom Ethan had armed were getting into positions along the uppermost ledge, trying to take aim on the abbies that were already climbing the wall.

Theresa watched one woman drop her rifle.

Saw a man lose his footing and fall screaming into the forest.

The first gunshot rang out from the ledge.

"Mom, what do we do?"

Theresa hated the terror she saw building in

Ben's eyes. She glanced back at the rocky path leading into the cavern.

"Should we have stayed inside?" Ben asked.

"And prayed the door held? No."

To the right of the cave opening, a narrow ledge extended around the mountain. From this distance, Theresa couldn't tell if it was navigable, but it was something.

"Come on." She grabbed Ben's arm and hustled him back up the path toward the tunnel as more gunshots broke out behind them.

"I thought you said—"

"We aren't going back into the cavern, Ben."

When they reached the opening to the tunnel, Theresa got her first good look at the ledge. It couldn't have been wider than a foot. There were no planks, no cables. It looked right on the edge of plausible.

She faced her son as people streaked past them, heading back into the tunnel.

Somewhere in the forest below, an abby shrieked.

"We have to follow this ledge," she said.

Ben stared at the slim, natural path across the cliff face, and said, "That looks scary."

"Would you rather be trapped in that cavern when fifty abbies break the door down?"

"What about everyone else?"

"My job is to protect you. You ready?"

He gave a quick, unconvincing nod.

Theresa felt her stomach clench. She stepped out onto the ledge and pressed her chest against the wall, her palms trailing across the rock. Taking small, shuffling steps, she clutched handholds where she could find them. After five feet, she looked back at Ben.

"See how I did that?"

"Yeah."

"Your turn."

Hard as it had been leaving the safety of that wide path into the mountain, it was infinitely more excruciating to watch her son step out onto the ledge. The very first thing he did was look down.

"No, don't do that, honey. Look at me."

Ben looked up. "It's a lot scarier in the daylight."

"Just focus on taking safe steps, and keep your hands on the wall like I am. Sometimes there will be places to grab."

Ben started toward her, step by step.

"You're doing great, honey."

He reached her.

They went on.

After twenty feet, the exposure opened up wide beneath them, a four-hundred-foot drop straight down to the forest floor. So vertical, if you fell you wouldn't bounce off anything until you hit the ground.

"How we doing, buddy?" Theresa asked.

"Okay."

"Are you looking down?"

"No."

Theresa glanced back. He was.

"Goddammit, Ben."

"I can't help it," he said. "It makes my stomach feel weird and tingly."

She wanted to reach out, take his hand, hold him tight.

"We need to keep moving," she said.

Theresa couldn't be certain, but the path seemed to be narrowing. Her left foot, which she kept perpendicular to the ledge and pointed into the mountain, was hanging off the edge by an inch or two.

As they arrived at a bend in the mountain, a flurry of gunfire exploded back toward the cavern. Theresa and Ben both looked. Several dozen people were retreating up the path into the tunnel with a speed and intensity that suggested they were fleeing for their lives. The scream of an abby, and another, and another broke out as those pale, translucent monsters climbed off the side of the cliff wall. When they got their talons on level ground, the abbies rushed on all fours up the path toward the tunnel.

"What if they see us?" Ben asked.

"Don't move," Theresa whispered. "Not even a muscle."

When the last of the abbies—she counted

forty-four—had disappeared into the tunnel, Theresa said, "Let's go."

As they moved around the bend, a deep, thumping sound spilled out of the tunnel.

"What is that?" Ben asked.

"The abbies. They're beating on the door to the cavern."

Theresa hugged the cliff and stepped around the corner onto a six-inch ledge, her heart in her throat.

Suddenly, a great chorus of screams rose up inside the tunnel.

HASSLER

GAS WORKS PARK
SEATTLE, WASHINGTON
1,816 YEARS AGO

Hassler flips burgers on a grill in the shadow of the remnants of the Seattle Gas Light Company, a collection of rusted cylinders and ironwork that looms in the distance like the ruins of a steampunk skyline. The expanse of emerald grass runs down to the edge of Lake Union, which sparkles under the late afternoon sun. It's June. It's warm. The entire city seems to be out taking advantage of this rare, perfect day.

Sailboat masts add triangles of color to the lake.

Kites sprinkle color in the sky.

Frisbees slice through the air and the bright noise of children's laughter echoes from the plant's exhauster-compressor building, which has been renovated into a "play barn."

It's the annual company picnic for the Secret Service's Seattle field office, and

Hassler can't shake how odd it is to see his team sporting all those bare legs and sandaled feet in place of crisp black suits and pantsuits.

His assistant, Mike, walks up carrying two empty plates and a couple of bratwurst requests.

As Hassler spears one of the brats, he spots Theresa Burke moving away from the group she's been standing with, heading down toward the shoreline at a pace substantially faster than a leisurely stroll.

Hassler sets down the fork and looks at his assistant.

"Did I mention I'm promoting you?" Hassler says.

Mike's eyes go wide with self-interest. The young man has only been working with Hassler for eight months, but he has, on a number of occasions, demonstrated a complete lack of awareness regarding the fact that his main purpose in life is answering the phones, pouring coffee, and typing up the special agent in charge's dictation.

Mike says, "Seriously?"

Hassler lifts the white-and-red checkerboard apron over his head and appoints his apprentice.

"Your new duties include asking people if they'd like a hamburger, bratwurst, or both. And also, not burning shit."

Mike's shoulders sag. "I was getting a plate for Lacy."

"That your new girl?"

"Yeah."

"Tell her to come over so you can fill her in on the big news." Hassler slaps Mike on the shoulder and abandons the grill, moving down through the buttercup-dotted grass.

Theresa stands by the water.

Hassler walks to the shore and stops twenty feet away, pretending to take in the splendor of the view.

The radio towers at the top of Capitol Hill.

The house-covered hillsides of Queen Anne.

After a moment, he glances over.

Theresa stares hard across the water, her jaw tight, eyes intense.

He asks, "Everything okay?"

She startles, looks over, wipes her eyes, and musters up a pathetic smile.

"Oh, yeah. Just enjoying the day. Wish we got more like this."

"No kidding. Kind of makes me wish I knew how to sail."

Theresa glances back toward the park where the rest of the party is mingling.

Hassler looks too.

The breeze carries the pleasant reek of beer in plastic cups.

He spots Ethan Burke and Kate Hewson standing off to the side, just the two of them, Kate laughing as Ethan gestures his way through what appears to be a story or a joke.

Hassler closes the distance between himself and Theresa.

"You're not having much fun, are you?"

She shakes her head.

Hassler says, "These work parties must be weird for the families. My agents see each other day in, day out. Probably spend more time together than with their own spouses. Then you come here, feel like an outsider."

Theresa smiles. "You pretty much nailed it."

She starts to say something else, but stops short.

"What?" Hassler prods, venturing a step closer. He can smell her conditioner, whatever body wash she used that morning.

Theresa's eyes are clear and green. The electricity goes in through his eyes and travels down into the pit of his stomach. He feels, all at once—sick, exhilarated, terrified, alive.

Radiantly so.

"Should I be worried?" she asks.

"Worried?"

She lowers her voice. "About them. Ethan and"—it's like she doesn't even want to say the word, like it brings a bad taste to her mouth—"Kate."

"Worried how?"

He knows. He just wants to hear her say it.

"They've been partners, what? Four months now?" she asks.

"Yeah, something like that."

"That's an intense relationship, right? Partner-partner?"

"Can be. You work cases together. Often long hours. You have to trust each other with your lives."

"So she's like his work wife."

Hassler says, "I'd be hard-pressed to name any pair of agents under my supervision who aren't close. The nature of the job pushes people together."

"It's just hard," Theresa says.

"I can't imagine."

"So you don't think . . ."

"I haven't personally seen anything that

would make me suspect Ethan is anything other than a devoted husband to you. He's a lucky man. I hope you know that."

Theresa blows out a sigh, puts her face into her hands.

"What's wrong?" he asks.

"I shouldn't have—"

"No, it's fine. Please."

"Do me a favor?" Theresa asks.

"Name it."

"Don't tell Ethan about this conversation. You don't know me that well, Adam, but I'm not a jealous person. It's just . . . I don't know what's wrong with me."

"Lips are sealed." Hassler smiles. "And you should know, I'm pretty good with the whole confidentiality thing. The word 'secret' is in my job title, for chrissakes."

Now Theresa smiles at him and he can barely stand it, knows he will think of little else in the days to come.

"Thank you," she says, and puts her hand briefly on his arm.

He could live a year in this moment.

"I could stay here," he offers. "Keep you company . . ."

"Oh no, you've got a party to get back to, and I've got some big girl panties to pull up. But you're sweet to offer."

Theresa starts back up the grassy slope and Hassler watches her go. What it is about this woman that rips his heart out, he can't exactly say. Truth be told, they're just acquaintances. Have talked only a handful of times.

When she breezed through the office to bring Ethan something.

A bump-into-each-other at the symphony.

A cookout he was invited to at the Burke house.

Hassler has never been married, hasn't been in love since high school, but in this moment, as he stands on the shore of Lake Union watching Theresa arrive at Ethan's side and wrap her arm around his waist, he feels a flicker of blinding jealousy, as if he's watching the woman who belongs with him falling for another man.

ETHAN

He crashed the CJ-5 through the rock-facade door. A piece of metal struck the windshield, sent a long, branching crack straight down the middle of the glass.

Ethan had half expected a brigade of Pilcher's men to be waiting for him, but the tunnel stood empty.

He shifted into third gear.

Thirty-five miles per hour up the steep grade was the best he could do.

Lights streamed past overhead.

The bedrock dripping on the fractured windshield.

Every time he rounded a curve, he expected to see a roadblock, a line of Pilcher's men with assault rifles and orders to shoot on sight.

Then again, it was possible Pilcher's people had no idea what he'd done.

The only camera feeds in the superstructure were in surveillance HQ and Pilcher's office. Surveillance techs could be sealed off, locked up, bribed, killed. Pilcher's inner circle no doubt held a delusional sense of loyalty toward the man, but Ethan couldn't let himself imagine all of them just standing by while he murdered the last of humanity.

His ears popped.

He was getting close and still no sign of resistance.

If he had to bet, Pilcher was planning to make certain that every last resident of Wayward Pines had been wiped out and then tell his people there had been a terrible accident. A fence failure. Nothing to be done.

Ethan eased his foot off the gas as the entrance to the superstructure came into view around a long, gentle curve.

He rolled into the massive cavern and brought the Jeep to a stop.

Jammed the gearshift into first.

Killed the engine.

He picked the Desert Eagle up off the floorboard, tugged the slide back and let it reset so the gun looked loaded. Digging through his pockets again, he only found two boxes of twelve-gauge slugs and his Harpy.

Opening the door, he stepped down onto the stone. The ark was quiet, no sound but a soft hiss—the rush of forced air—coming from the blue-lit suspension center.

Ethan unzipped his parka and tossed it into the Jeep, shoved the impotent Desert Eagle down the front of his mud-smeared, bloodstained Wranglers.

Approaching the thick glass doors that led into Level 1 of the complex, it dawned on him that he didn't have a keycard.

A camera pointed down at him from above the doors.

Are you watching me now?

You must know I'm here.

A voice behind him said, "Put your hands on your head. Interlock your fingers."

Ethan raised his hands and turned slowly.

A kid in his early twenties with a bandage around his head stood fifty feet away beside the closest of the massive cylindrical reservoirs in the ark, pointing an AR-15 at Ethan.

"Hi, Marcus," Ethan said.

Marcus moved toward him, and in the jaundiced illumination of the hanging globe lights, looked mad as hell. To be fair, he had cause. During their last encounter, Ethan had pistol-whipped him.

"Mr. Pilcher knew you'd come," Marcus said.

"He told you that, huh?"

"He told me everything you did."

"Everything I did?"

"And he also told me to shoot you, so—"

"People are dying in Wayward Pines, Marcus. Women. Children."

Marcus had halved the distance between them and Ethan could read enough rage in his eyes to suggest he might actually pull the trigger.

The glass doors opened. Ethan glanced back, saw a big blond man enter, aiming a pistol at his heart. Ethan remembered him from that day in the morgue. Alyssa's friend, Alan—Pilcher's head of security.

Ethan looked at Marcus, the kid now shouldering the machine gun, preparing to shoot.

Ethan said to Alan, "You have orders to shoot me on sight as well?"

"Better believe."

"Where's Ted?"

"No idea."

"You might want to hear me out first," Ethan said.

Marcus was closing in. As Alan pointed his pistol in Ethan's face, Marcus reached forward and tugged the Desert Eagle out of Ethan's waistband, threw it across the stone.

"You have no idea what's going on out there," Ethan said. "Either of you. Last night, Pilcher turned off the fence and opened the gate. He let a swarm of abbies into the valley. Most of the town has been massacred."

"Bullshit," Alan said.

"He's lying," Marcus said. "Why are we even listening—"

Ethan said, "I want to show you something. I'm reaching slowly into my pocket—"

Alan said, "I swear to God that'll be the last move you ever make."

"You just took my weapon."

Marcus said, "Alan, we have orders. I—"

"Shut the fuck up," Ethan said. "Adults are

talking." He looked back at Alan. "Remember when we met in the morgue? Remember what you asked me to do?"

"Find who killed Alyssa."

"That's right."

Alan fixed his eyes on Ethan.

"I found who killed her," Ethan said.

Alan's jaw tensed.

"It was your boss. And Pam."

Alan said, "You come in here with an accusation like that you better be able to—"

"Prove it?" Ethan pointed at his pocket. "May I?"

"Slowly."

Ethan reached in, fingers probing until he felt it. Lifting out the memory shard, he held up the square shaving of metal, and said, "Pilcher and Pam killed Alyssa. But first they tortured her. The head of surveillance gave this to me. It shows everything." Alan kept the gun trained on Ethan, his expression unreadable. "I have a question for you, Alan," Ethan said. "If what I'm telling you is true, where does your loyalty fall?"

"He's playing you," Marcus growled.

"One way to find out," Ethan said. "What does it cost you to look at this, Alan? Unless avenging Alyssa isn't something that interests you."

Behind the glass doors, Ethan saw another armed man sprinting down the corridor.

He was dressed in black, armed with a Taser, pistol, machine gun, and testosterone. As he approached the glass doors, he spotted Ethan and raised his weapon. Alan suddenly wrapped his right arm around Ethan's neck and held his pistol to Ethan's temple.

The doors whisked open.

Alan said, "I've got him. Stand down."

"Kill him!" Marcus screamed. "You have orders!"

The new arrival said, "Alan, what the hell are you doing?"

"You do not want to shoot this man, Mustin. Not yet."

"What I want and don't want doesn't have a whole helluva lot to do with it. You know that better than any of us."

Alan tightened his grip on Ethan.

"Sheriff says the town's been overrun with aberrations and that the bossman opened up the gate. He also says that Mr. Pilcher and Pam are responsible for Alyssa's death."

"One thing to say it," Mustin said. "Another to prove it."

Ethan held up the memory shard.

"He claims it has footage of Alyssa's death."

"So what?" Marcus said.

Alan leveled a wilting glare at the young man. "What are you saying, son? That on the wild assumption any of this is true, you'd be a-okay with Mr. Pilcher killing one of our own, his own daughter, and trying to hide it? You'd just go along with that?"

"He's the boss," Marcus said. "If he did something like that, I bet he had—"

"He's not God, is he?"

A scream raced up the tunnel and went reverberating through the ark.

Alan released Ethan and said, "What was that?"

"Sounds like some of the abbies found their way into the mountain," Ethan said. "I drove through the entrance to the tunnel."

Alan looked at Mustin's weapon. "What do we have that's meaner than an AR-15?"

"An M230 chain gun on a rolling mount."

"Mustin, Marcus, get on that chain gun. Call everybody up. The entire team."

"What are you going to do with him?" Marcus asked, jutting his chin toward Ethan.

"He and I are heading up to surveillance to take a look at what he's got."

"We were told to kill him," Marcus said, raising his gun.

Alan stepped toward Marcus, the barrel of the AR-15 digging into his sternum.

"Would you mind not pointing your weapon at me, son?"

Marcus lowered his gun.

"While you and Mustin make sure we don't all

get eaten, I'm going to look at what the sheriff says is proof concerning what happened to my friend. And if it's anything less than advertised, I'll execute him on the spot. That all right with you?"

THERESA

"You're almost there!" Theresa whispered.

Ben lowered his shoe toward the next foothold.

The cries and the screams from the Wanderers' cavern were still audible. That narrow ledge had just run out, and now they were down-climbing a fifty-degree stretch of cliff. So far, the abundance of handholds and footholds in the good, hard granite had saved their lives, but Theresa couldn't ignore the two-hundred-foot fall that awaited the slightest misstep. The reality that her son was on this rock wall with her was almost too much to bear.

If Ben fell, she'd jump right after him.

But so far, he was listening, following her instructions, and doing a damn fine job of holding his twelve-year-old shit together.

Ben stepped down onto the ledge where Theresa had been perched for the last few minutes. It didn't lead anywhere, but at least there was enough of a surface so they didn't have to cling desperately to a handhold.

They still had a long way to go, but progress had been made, and the tops of the pine trees were only twenty feet below them.

Another scream broke out of the tunnel far above.

"Don't think about it," Theresa said. "Don't imagine what they're going through. Just focus on where you are, Ben. On making smart, safe moves."

"Everyone in that cave is going to die," he said.

"Ben—"

"If we hadn't found the ledge—"

"But we did. And soon we're going to get off this cliff and find your father."

"Are you scared?" he asked.

"Of course I am."

"Me too."

Theresa reached over and touched her son's face. It was slick and cool with sweat and rosy with exertion and the beginnings of a sunburn.

"Do you think Dad's okay?" Ben asked.

"I think he is," she said, but her eyes filled with tears at the thought of Ethan. "Your old man's one tough hombre. I hope you know that."

Ben nodded, glanced down the face of the cliff into the welcoming darkness of the dense pine forest.

"I don't want to get eaten," he said.

"We're not. We're tough hombres too. We're a family of tough hombres."

"You're not a tough hombre," Ben said.

"Excuse me?"

"You're a tough *hombra*."

Theresa rolled her eyes and said, "Come on, brat. We better keep moving."

• • •

It was late afternoon when they stepped from the rock onto the soft floor of the forest.

They had been on the cliff for hours, under the burn of direct sunlight. They dripped sweat as their eyes readjusted in the cool shadow of the trees.

"What now?" Ben asked.

Theresa wasn't sure exactly. By her estimate, they were approximately a mile from the edge of town, but she wasn't confident that heading for Wayward Pines was the safest play. The abbies wanted to feed. They would stay where the people were, or at least where they'd been. Then again, if she and Ben made it into town, they could hole up inside a house. Lock themselves into a basement. If the abbies found them in the forest, there'd be nowhere to hide. It was already getting late, and she didn't relish the thought of sleeping out here in the woods, in the dark.

Theresa said, "I think we go back into town."

"But that's where the abbies are."

"I know of a place where we can hide. Wait this out until your dad fixes it."

Theresa started off into the trees, Ben following close on her heels.

"Why are you going so slowly?" he asked.

"Because we don't want to step on any branches. We don't want to make a sound. If

228

something comes our way, we need to be able to hear it early enough to hide."

They went on, winding their way down through the trees.

They heard no more screams, human or abby.

Nothing but their own footsteps in the pine needles, their heavy exhalations, and the whoosh of wind pushing through the tops of the trees.

ETHAN

He followed Alan through the glass doors. They took the stairwell up to the second floor, came off the landing, and headed down the corridor into Level 2.

As they approached surveillance, Alan pulled a keycard out of his pocket.

When he swiped it at the door, a red dot lit up above the reader.

Alan tried again, same result.

He banged on the door.

"It's Alan Spear. Open up."

No answer.

Alan stepped back, fired four rounds into the card reader, and then put a size thirteen boot into the center of the door.

It burst open.

Ethan let Alan move in first.

The room was dark, illuminated only by the glow from the wall of monitors.

No one at the console.

Ethan waited in the threshold as Alan approached the inner door.

He tried his keycard again: green light.

Dead bolt retracting.

Alan pointed his AR-15 into the side room.

"Clear!" he said.

Ethan walked in, and asked, "Can you operate this system?"

"I can figure out how to play that memory shard. Give it here."

They sat at the console.

As Alan slipped the shard into a port, Ethan looked up at the screens.

All were dark but one.

A camera feed showed the school basement—a large crowd packed into a classroom. In the center of the room, the injured lay on makeshift cots while neighbors tended to them and nursed their wounds. He searched for Kate but couldn't pick her out.

An image appeared on another screen.

It was a long camera view across a field—the riverside park. It showed a man limping beside the river.

Ethan said, "Look, Alan."

Alan looked up.

The man on the screen began to run—the awkward, stumbling gait of someone who'd been wounded.

Three abbies sprinted into view on the left side of the screen as the man disappeared out of the right.

A new monitor flashed to life—a feed looking down Sixth Street, Ethan's street. The man ran out of the field and into the road, the abbies in pursuit, upright, all four of them moving closer and closer to the camera.

They ran him down in front of Ethan's house and killed him in the street.

Ethan felt a surge of nausea. Rage.

"I wondered this morning if something was up," Alan said.

"Why's that?"

"Mustin, that guard back there? He's a sniper. All day every day, he sits on top of a mountain overlooking the town and the canyon and shoots any abbies that try to come in. I saw him in the chow hall this morning when he should've been at his post. He said Pilcher had pulled him off the peak for today. No reason given. It was a clear day too."

"So Mustin wouldn't see what his boss had done to all those innocent people."

"When did they breach the fence?" Alan asked.

"Last night. You weren't told?"

"Not a word."

A new screen flared to life.

"That's the memory shard file?" Ethan asked.

"Yep. Have you seen this?"

"I have."

"And?"

"You can't unwatch it."

Alan played the file.

From high in the corner of a ceiling, a camera looked down on the morgue. There was Pilcher.

Pam. And Alyssa. The young woman had been strapped with thick, leather restraints to the autopsy table.

"No audio?" Alan asked.

"It's a good thing."

Alyssa was screaming, her head lifting off the table, every muscle straining.

Pam appeared, took a handful of Alyssa's hair, and jerked her head down against the metal table.

When David Pilcher moved into frame, set a small knife on the metal table, and climbed on top of Alyssa, Ethan looked away.

He'd seen this once before, didn't need the images reinforced inside his brain.

Alan said, "Jesus God."

He stopped the video, pushed his chair back from the console, and stood.

"Where are you going?" Ethan asked.

"Where do you think?" He moved toward the door.

"Wait."

"What?" Alan glanced back. You wouldn't have known what he'd just seen to look at his face. That Nordic iciness as blank as a winter sky.

"The people in town need you right now," Ethan said.

"I'm going to go kill him first if that's okay with you."

"You're not thinking."

"His own *daughter!*"

233

"He's done," Ethan said. "Finished. But he has information we're going to need. Go mobilize your men. Send a team to shut the gate and restore power to the fence. I'll go to Pilcher."

"*You* will."

Ethan stood. "That's right."

Alan dug his keycard out of his pocket, dropped it on the floor, and said, "You'll need this."

A key fell beside the card.

"That too. It's for the elevator. And while we're at it . . ." He pulled a subcompact Glock out of a shoulder holster, held it by the barrel, and offered Ethan the gun. As Ethan took it, Alan said, "If the next time I see you, you confess that, in the heat of the moment, you put a round into that piece of shit's gut and watched as he bled out slowly, I will totally understand."

"I'm sorry about Alyssa."

Alan left the room.

Ethan bent down, lifted the key and the plastic card off the floor.

The corridor was empty.

Halfway down the stairwell, he heard it.

A noise he knew all too well from his time at war.

They were firing the chain gun, and it sounded like death on the drums.

By the time he reached Level 1, the noise was unreal. People would be leaving their workstations, leaving their residences.

At the pair of unmarked doors, he swiped the card through the reader.

The doors opened.

He stepped into the small elevator car, pushed the key into the lock on the control panel, and turned it.

The single button started blinking.

He pressed it, the doors closed, and the racket of the chain gun began to gradually fade away.

He took a deep breath and thought of his family, his fear for them blooming in his stomach like a flower of broken glass.

The doors opened.

He stepped off into Pilcher's suite.

Passing the kitchen, he heard the sizzle of meat cooking. Garlic, onions, olive oil perfuming the air, Chef Tim obliviously at work while the abbies invaded, intently plating Pilcher's breakfast, adding intricate dots of a bright red sauce from a pastry bag onto a piece of china.

As Ethan moved down the hall toward Pilcher's office, he checked the load on Alan's Glock, happy to see a round already in the tube.

He opened the doors to Pilcher's office without bothering to knock, and strode inside.

Pilcher sat on one of the leather sofas that faced the wall of monitors, feet propped up on an acacia wood coffee table, a remote control in one hand, a bottle of something old and brown in the other.

The left side of the wall showed feeds from Wayward Pines.

The right—surveillance from inside the super-structure.

Ethan walked over to the sofa, took a seat beside him. He could break Pilcher's neck. Beat him to death. Suffocate him. The only thing stopping him really was the sense that this man's death belonged mostly to the people of Wayward Pines. He couldn't steal that away from them. Not after everything Pilcher had put them through.

Pilcher looked over, his face streaked with deep scratch marks that still oozed blood.

"Who'd you tangle with?" Ethan asked.

"I had to let Ted go this morning."

Ethan bristled.

Pilcher smelled boozy. He wore a black satin robe and looked disheveled as hell as he offered Ethan the bottle.

"No thanks."

On one of the screens, Ethan saw the brilliant muzzle flash of the chain gun cutting down abbies in the tunnel.

On another—abbies on Main Street, lacka-daisically feeding on kills from the night before, their stomachs bulging.

"Quite an end to it all," Pilcher said.

"Nothing's ending but you."

"I don't blame you," Pilcher said.

"Blame me? For what?"

"Your envy."

"What exactly do you think I envy?"

"Me, of course. The way it feels to sit behind that desk. To have . . . created all of this."

"You think that's all this is about? That I want your job?"

"I know you believe in your heart it's about giving people truth and freedom, but the truth, Ethan, is there is nothing in this world like power. The power to kill. To spare." He waved at the screens. "To control lives. To make them better. Or worse. If there ever was a God I think I know how he must have felt. People demanding answers they could never handle. People hating him even as they basked in the safety he provided. I think I finally understand why God went away and left the world to destroy itself." Pilcher smiled. "And you will too one day, Ethan. After you've sat behind that desk for a while. You'll understand that the people in that valley aren't like you and me. They can't handle what you told them last night. You'll see."

"Maybe, maybe not. Either way, they deserved to know the truth."

"I'm not saying it was perfect. Or even fair. But before you came, Ethan, it worked. I protected these people and they lived the closest thing to normal lives that they could ever hope for. I gave them a beautiful town and the opportunity to have faith that all was as it should be."

Pilcher drank straight from the bottle.

"Your fatal flaw, Ethan, is that you're under the mistaken impression that people are like you. That they have your courage, your fearlessness, your will. You and I are exceptions, cut from the same cloth. Even my people in the mountain struggle with the fear. But not you and me. We know the truth. We aren't afraid to look it in the eye. Only difference being, I'm aware of this fact, and it's something you're going to learn slowly and painfully and at great cost of human life. But you'll remember this conversation one day, Ethan. You'll understand why I did the things I did."

"I'll never understand why you turned off the fence. Why you murdered your daughter."

"Rule long enough, you will."

"I don't plan on ruling."

"No?" Pilcher laughed. "What do you think you've got down there? Plymouth Rock? You going to write a constitution? Start a democracy? The world beyond the fence is too cruel, too hostile. That town needs one strong man to lead."

"Why did you turn off the fence, David?"

The old man sipped his whiskey.

"Without me, this would be a world free of our species. We're here because of me and me alone. My money. My brilliance. My vision. I gave them *everything*."

"Why did you do it?"

"You might as well say I created them. And you. And you have the gall to ask—"

"Why?"

Pilcher's eyes suddenly burned with unchecked rage.

"Where were they when I discovered that the human genome was becoming corrupted? That humanity would become extinct in a matter of generations? When I built a thousand suspended animation units? When I dug a tunnel into the heart of a mountain and stocked a five-million-square-foot ark with enough supplies to rebuild the last town on earth? And while we're on the topic, Ethan: *Where the fuck were you?*"

Pilcher's entire body shook with fury.

"Were you there the day I emerged from suspended animation and took my crew outside to find that the abbies had taken over the world? Were you there as I walked down Main Street watching my workers frame each building? Pave each road? On the morning I called the head of suspension into this office and instructed him to wake you up so you could be with your wife and son again? I gave you this life, Ethan. You and everyone in that valley. Everyone in this mountain."

"Why?"

He growled, "Because I could. Because I am

239

their fucking creator, and creations don't get to question the one who made them. Who gives them breath. And who can, at any second, snatch it all away."

Ethan looked up at the monitors. They showed chaos in the cavern. The chain gun was empty and the guards were falling back with their AR-15s as the monsters advanced.

"I didn't have to even let you up here. I could've locked the elevator. What are you going to do with me?" Pilcher asked quietly.

"That's for the people you tried to murder to decide."

Pilcher's eyes misted.

As if, for a fleeting moment, he saw himself with clarity.

He looked back at his desk.

At the wall of screens.

His voice became raspy with emotion.

"It got away from me," he said, and then he blinked, a hardness returning to those small black eyes, like water freezing over.

Pilcher came at Ethan with a short-bladed fighting knife, a sudden, lunging stab aimed straight at Ethan's gut.

Ethan deflected Pilcher's wrist, the blade only grazing his side.

Rising to his feet, he rained down a savage left hook that snapped Pilcher's head around and cracked his cheekbone, the force of the blow driving him off the couch, his head smashing into the edge of the coffee table.

Pilcher shivered out on his back and the knife slipped out of his grasp, clattering to the hardwood floor.

HASSLER

SECRET SERVICE HQ
SEATTLE, WASHINGTON
1,814 YEARS AGO

Hassler enters his corner office in the Columbia Center, happy to see Ethan Burke already seated across from his desk. By his watch, he's five minutes late. Burke probably arrived five minutes early, which means he's been waiting at least ten minutes.

Good.

"Sorry to keep you waiting," Hassler says as he walks past his agent.

"Not a problem."

"Imagine you're wondering why I pulled you off that Everett thing."

"We're close to an arrest."

"That's good to hear, but I have something more pressing for you."

Hassler takes a seat and studies Ethan across the desk. He isn't wearing his black-and-whites today. His surveillance outfit is a gray jumpsuit, the shoulders still damp from the late-morning drizzle. He can just see the outline on Ethan's left side of his concealed shoulder holster.

It crosses Hassler's mind that he can still pull the plug on this. Until the words leave his mouth, he hasn't committed a crime.

In his years in law enforcement, interrogating criminals, he's always hearing about the nebulous line between right and wrong. They were only stealing for their family. They'd only intended to do it once. And his favorite: they didn't even realize they'd crossed a line until they were deep into enemy territory on the other side, with no hope of ever getting back.

But as Hassler sits on this side of the desk, this side of the line, all that conjecture on the ambiguous nature of right and wrong feels like bullshit.

He sees his choice with crystalline clarity.

If he sends Ethan on this assignment, he has crossed the line forever.

No coming back.

If he ejects out of this entire enterprise, lets Ethan go back to his case in Everett, he stays a good guy who almost did a very bad thing.

Nothing confusing here. No gray area from his perspective.

"Sir?" Ethan says.

Hassler pictures Theresa, a couple years back at the company picnic. Thinks of Ethan flirting with Kate while his wife cried by herself on the shore of Lake Union.

Theresa's fears about Kate and Ethan were borne out last year when Kate put in an abrupt transfer request for Boise, Idaho. Ethan cheated on Theresa with his partner, and everyone knew it. He humiliated his wife, and a woman like Theresa deserves so much better.

"Adam?" Ethan says.

Hassler lets out a breath as rain ticks on the window behind him.

He says, "Kate Hewson is missing."

Ethan leans forward in the chair. "For how long?"

"Four days."

"She went missing on the job?"

"Her partner's missing too. Guy named Evans. You and Kate had a . . . special relationship, right?"

Ethan doesn't bite, just stares, intense.

"Well, I just figured you'd want to take on the search for your old partner."

Ethan stands.

"Boise is e-mailing the case file," Hassler says. "We're booking you on a flight out of Sea-Tac first thing. Tomorrow morning, you'll meet up with Agent Stallings in the Boise field office and the two of you will head north to the last place anyone heard from Kate."

"Where's that?"

"Little town called Wayward Pines."

Hassler watches Ethan leave.

He's done it.

Set it all in motion.

And the weird thing is, he doesn't feel any different. No regret, no fear, no anxiety.

If there's one overriding emotion, it's relief.

Spinning around in his chair, he stares out his window at the gray, wet gloom of downtown Seattle, the water droplets beading and running down the glass.

From his office on the thirty-first floor, he can see the building where Theresa works as a paralegal. Imagines her sitting in her lifeless cube, typing dictation.

He doesn't know how exactly, but he will have her one day. He'll love her like she's meant to be loved. Somehow, and this is the biggest mystery of his entire existence, she has become the only thing that matters in his world.

Flipping open his prepaid cell phone, he dials.

David Pilcher answers, "Hello?"

"It's me," Hassler says.

"I was beginning to wonder if I'd ever hear from you again."

"He's coming to you tomorrow."

"We'll be ready."

Hassler closes the cell, takes out the battery, and breaks the phone in half. He places the two pieces in the Styrofoam container at the bottom of his trash can that holds the remnants of yesterday's lunch.

THERESA

Theresa and Ben reached the edge of the forest as the sun dipped behind the distant peaks.

She whispered to her son, "Wait here."

Moving on, Theresa crawled through a grove of scrub oak, the dead leaves crunching too loudly under her knees.

Where the oaks ended, she peered through the branches.

They had reached the outskirts of Wayward Pines but had somehow traversed the entire forest to the north side of town. The streets that Theresa could see appeared empty. The houses dark. And not a murmur to be heard.

She glanced back at Ben, waved him over.

He crawled noisily through the leaves and squatted down beside her.

Putting her mouth to his ear, she whispered, "We need to travel ten blocks."

"Where are we going?"

"Sheriff's station."

"Walk or run?"

"Run," Theresa whispered. "But take a few breaths first, fill those lungs up with air."

She and Ben both drew in deep pulls of oxygen.

"Ready?" she asked.

"Ready."

Theresa scrambled out of the thicket and climbed to her feet, then turned and helped Ben up off the ground. They stood in the backyard of a Victorian she recognized—she'd sold this house to a young, expecting couple three months ago after their good behavior in town had been rewarded with an upgrade to a larger, nicer home.

What had been their fate these last twenty-four hours of hell?

Most front yards in Wayward Pines were enclosed by white picket fences, so she and Ben jogged up the sidewalk.

The valley was going dark.

Night always seemed to set in a little too quickly once the sun had gone behind the mountains, and considering there was no power in the entire valley, this would be a black evening.

They were coming up on the first dead body in the street.

Theresa looked back at Ben, and said, "Don't look, honey."

But she didn't take her own advice.

The good news was that it had been eviscerated so completely it looked less like a human being than a pile of guts and bones. A buzzard roosted on the ribcage, glutting itself.

They reached the intersection of First Avenue and Eleventh Street.

Theresa could see the tall pine trees in the

251

distance that soared out of the front lawn of the sheriff's office.

"Almost there," she said. "Block and a half to go."

"I'm tired."

"I am too, but let's finish strong."

At the intersection of First and Thirteenth, Ben whispered, "Mom!"

"What?"

"Look!"

Theresa glanced back.

Three blocks down Thirteenth Street, two pale forms were running on all fours in their direction.

"Sprint!" Theresa screamed.

They accelerated, a surge of adrenaline-boosting power and speed. She leapt over the curb and raced up through the trimmed grass toward the entrance to the sheriff's office.

Once inside, Theresa stopped and looked back through the glass doors toward the street.

"Did they see us come in here?" Ben asked.

The first abby hit the intersection at full speed, and without missing a beat, altered its course, now heading straight for the sheriff's office.

"Come on!" Theresa wheeled around and bolted through the lobby.

The farther they moved away from the entrance, the darker it got.

Crossing the threshold, she turned the corner

into Ethan's office, saw the gun cabinet wide open, ammunition spilled across the floor, several rifles left behind on the desk.

The bottom cabinets of the gun case were open too.

She reached inside, pulled out a large pistol, pointed it at the wall, and squeezed the trigger. Nothing happened. The safety was on or it wasn't loaded or both.

"Hurry, Mom!"

She grabbed a revolver out of the case but it was empty, and she didn't even know how to break the cylinder open to load it assuming she could even match up the right ammo. From where she crouched by the gun case, there were at least half a dozen different sizes of cartridges scattered across the floor beneath her feet.

"Mom, what are you doing?" Ben asked.

This wasn't going to work. They were out of time, and despite being married to a Secret Service agent, she didn't know the first thing about firearms.

"New plan," she said.

"What?"

She jerked open Ethan's desk. It had to be there. His first week on the job, Ethan had given her a tour of this place, including locking her into the single jail cell as he swung the key on his finger by the carabiner it was attached to, smirking as he drawled, "Unless you can think of some way to bribe the sheriff, looks like you're spending a night in lockup, Mrs. Burke."

She'd seen him return that key to this middle desk drawer, and now she reached all the way to the back, fingers desperately searching.

There.

She felt the carabiner, pulled the key out, and rushed around the desk to Ben.

"What are we doing?" he asked.

"Just follow me!"

They tore back down the hallway.

An abby screamed outside.

"They're here, Mom!"

As they crossed the lobby, Theresa glanced toward the entrance, saw the pair of abbies running up the walkway lined with baby pine trees, seconds away from entering.

She shouted, "Faster, Ben!"

They turned down another dark hallway.

At the far end, Theresa saw the black bars of Wayward Pines's only jail cell.

First time she'd seen it, it had reminded her of the cells in *The Andy Griffith Show*. Something almost quaint about those vertical bars. The single bed and the desk inside. The kind of place where the Saturday-night drunks had a standing reservation.

Now, the cell looked like a life raft.

The hallway opened up at the end, the

fading evening light slanting in through a high window.

Theresa slammed hard into the cell bars as the abbies crashed through the glass doors into the station.

She clutched the key, worked it into the lock.

Talons clicked down the dark hallway behind them.

One of the abbies shrieked.

The dead bolt turned.

Theresa opened the door, and screamed, "Get in!"

Ben rushed into the cell as the first abby launched out of the corridor.

She stepped in, jerked the door closed, and locked it a half second before the abby rammed the bars.

Ben screamed.

As the first abby picked itself up off the floor, its partner crawled out of the hallway.

It was the first time Theresa had seen an abby up close.

The one that had crashed into the cell was huge and covered in gore.

Death emanated off its blood-soaked skin.

Ben's back was up against the wall, his eyes gone wide, a puddle forming under his feet.

"Can they get us in here?" he asked.

"I don't think so."

"Are you sure?"

"No."

When the second abby collided with the bars, the entire structure shook.

Theresa wrapped her arms around Ben as the first abby stood to its full five-and-a-half-foot height.

It cocked its head and watched them through the bars, milky eyes blinking, processing, problem-solving.

"What's that thing moving inside its chest?" Theresa whispered.

"That's its heart, Mom."

"How do you—" *Oh. Right*. He'd learned about them in school.

The heart beat rapidly, blurred and distorted through the layers of skin, as if Theresa were watching it through several inches of ice.

This one's legs were short, and standing straight, its arms reached all the way down to the floor. It slid its right arm between the bars—slim but rippled with muscle. It was over four feet long, and Theresa watched in horror as those black talons stretched across the floor of the cell.

"Get away!" she screamed.

The other abby came around the side of the cell and did the same. Its left arm was five feet long and when one of its talons grazed Ben's shoe, Theresa stomped on its claw.

The abby roared.

Theresa pulled Ben toward the corner farthest away from the bars, where they climbed up onto the metal bed frame.

"Are we going to die, Mom?"

"No."

Three new abbies emerged from the corridor and broke for the cell, screeching and hissing. There were more behind them, the noise in the room growing and growing.

Soon there were fifteen arms reaching through the bars, and more abbies hurling themselves at the cell.

Theresa sank down onto the bare mattress and held Ben tightly in her arms.

The light coming through the window had changed from blue to purple, the room becoming steadily darker.

She put her lips to Ben's ear and said over the noise of the monsters, "Think about another place, another time."

Ben trembled in her arms, and still more abbies streamed into the room.

Theresa stared up at that high window as the monsters shook the bars and crashed into them and reached their hideously long arms into the cell.

The last thing she saw as the light went away was the room beyond the bars packed wall to wall with abbies and one of them kneeling down in front of the lock, trying to dig its talon into the keyhole.

Suddenly there was nothing to see. Night had fallen over Wayward Pines.

And they were in the dark with monsters.

ETHAN

Ethan rode the elevator out of Pilcher's suite to the Level 1 corridor. As the elevator opened, he could still hear gunshots, but they were distant now.

He headed for the glass doors at the end of the hallway, pulling the pistol Alan had given him as he crossed through the threshold into the ark.

It looked as if most of Pilcher's inner circle had come down to see the source of all the commotion; at least a hundred people were milling about, confused and scared.

The gunshots were louder here, the reports issuing from somewhere deep in the tunnel that led down through the mountain into Wayward Pines.

There were dead abbies everywhere.

Piles of them in the tunnel.

Forty or fifty in the cavern.

Blood running in channels over the stone.

Five bodies, covered by sheets, lay in a row next to the entrance to suspension.

The smell of spent munitions was over-powering.

Alan came running out of the tunnel.

Ethan pushed toward him through the crowd,

saw Alan's face speckled with blood, his right arm torn open by what Ethan surmised was the slash of a talon.

The racket of an AR-15 fired up in the tunnel.

Followed by a scream.

"We're pushing them back," Alan said, "but there must've been two hundred abbies. I've lost men. The M230 is out of ammo. If we hadn't had the chain gun, this would have gone a whole lot worse. Where's Pilcher?"

"He's unconscious, tied up in his office."

"I'll send someone down for him." Alan's radio squeaked. He answered, "Alan. Over."

Mustin's voice crackled through the speaker, shouting above gunfire, "We just drove the last band out of the tunnel, but the door's compromised! Over."

Alan said, "I've already got a truck heading down to you with sheets of reinforced steel and a three-man team of metalworkers. They're going to weld the door shut. Over."

"Copy that, we'll hold the line! Out!"

Ethan said, "You can't seal that exit. We have to get to the people in the valley. My wife and son are down there."

"We will, but we need to regroup, reload. I lost eight men that I know of. If we're going to roll out in force into Wayward Pines, we better take every last weapon in our arsenal. We have to find more ammo for that chain gun." His eyes became grave as he said, "And we can't go out there at night."

"What are you saying?"

"It's already evening. It'll be dark long before we're ready to go. We'll head into town at first light."

"Tomorrow?"

"We aren't equipped to do battle at night."

"You think the unarmed people in that valley are? You think my wife and son—"

"We'd be slaughtered in the dark, and you know it. All that would happen is we'd lose the only chance we have of saving those people."

"Goddammit!"

"You think I don't want to scream into town right now, guns blazing?"

Ethan moved toward the tunnel.

"Where do you think you're going?" Alan called after him.

"To find my family."

"You go out there at night, the only thing that's going to happen is you'll get eaten. There's *hundreds* of those things out there."

Two steps into the tunnel, Ethan stopped.

"I can only imagine how you feel," Alan said. "If it were my family out there, you wouldn't be able to hold me back. But you're smarter than I am, Ethan. And certainly you understand that your death tonight on some suicide mission isn't going to save your family or anyone else's."

Damn.

He was right.

Ethan turned, blew out a hard, frustrated sigh.

He said, "So the residents of Wayward Pines get to spend another night in the dark, in the cold, with no food, no water, sharing that valley with a swarm of abbies."

Alan came toward him.

Ethan could hear, far down the tunnel, more gunshots.

Alan said, "Hopefully, those who survived the initial invasion have found safe places to hole up. Where's your family?"

"I left them in a cave, behind a locked door, halfway up a mountain."

"So they're safe then."

"I have no way of knowing that. There's a group in the school," Ethan said. "Down in the basement. Eighty, ninety people. What if we just—"

"Too. Risky. And you know it."

Ethan nodded. "What about the gate in the fence? Is it still wide open? Another thousand or thirty thousand abbies could just stroll right into our valley if they wanted?"

"I had the lead technician look into that. He says we can't turn on the fence from inside the superstructure."

"Why?"

"Apparently, Pilcher sabotaged the internal

system. Only way to power the fence back up and close the gate is through the manual override."

"And let me guess . . ."

"It's at the fence. Wouldn't be fun if it were easy, right?"

"I say we send someone," Ethan said. "Right now."

"There's a secret exit on the south side of the mountain. It's only a quarter mile from there to the fence."

"Send that technician and a couple of guards."

"Okay. But while I do that . . ." Alan glanced over his shoulder at the crowd of people who had wandered into the ark. "They don't know anything. They just heard gunshots and came down here to see what's going on."

"I'll talk to them," Ethan said.

He started toward the crowd.

Alan called after him, "Be gentle!"

"Why should I?"

"Because this is the only life they know, and you're getting ready to blow it all to pieces."

THERESA

She jerked awake, her eyes opening to total darkness.

Ben was stirring, mumbling, "No, no, no," in his sleep.

She shook him awake and whispered, "You're okay, buddy. Mama's got you."

It had been years since she'd uttered words like those to her son. Not since she'd been a young mother, rocking her baby boy to sleep, the window cracked in his nursery and the two of them lulled by the whisper of soft Seattle rain.

"What's happening?" Ben asked.

"We're still in the jail cell, but we're okay."

"Where are the monsters?"

It was unnervingly quiet, no sound of movement beyond the bars.

"I think they're gone for now."

"I'm really thirsty."

"I know, buddy. Me too."

"Isn't there a water cooler behind the front desk?"

"I think so."

"Maybe we could sneak out there, try to get—"

"Oh, I don't think that'd be such a hot idea, Benjamin," said a woman in the darkness on the other side of the bars.

264

Theresa recoiled. "Who's there?"

"Don't you recognize my voice, honey? How could you not? You've been spilling your guts to me every fourth Thursday of the month for the last—"

"Pam? Oh my God, what are you—"

"I heard you two screaming a few hours ago, saw those abbies chase you into the sheriff's station. I waited until they left. I'm so relieved to find you both intact. You have no idea. That was quick thinking, Theresa, locking yourself in here."

Theresa had expected some level of sight to return, but she still couldn't see her hand in front of her face.

Pam said, "I'm not quite clear on what happened here last night. Did your husband show an abby to the town?"

"He told them everything. About the abbies. The surveillance. That it's two thousand years in the future. That we're all that's left."

"So he really did it. That motherfucker. Hey, don't look at me like that."

Theresa felt a cold knot ratcheting down in the small of her back.

"It's pitch black in here," Theresa said.

"Yes. It is. But I can see you holding Benjamin in your arms and glaring into the dark in the general vicinity of where I'm sitting, and I don't appreciate—"

"How?"

"They're called night-vision goggles, Theresa, and this isn't the first time I've watched you through them."

"What's she talking about, Mom?"

"Ben, don't—"

"Benjamin, I'm talking about the time I caught your mother and father sneaking out of your home on Sixth Street, after dark. That's strictly forbidden, you know."

"Don't speak like that to my son—"

"Don't speak like that to the woman who's pointing a twelve gauge at you."

For a moment, it was absolutely silent, Theresa trying to piece together the image—Pam sitting in front of their cell wearing night-vision goggles and aiming a shotgun at her and Ben in the dark.

"You're pointing a weapon at my son?" Theresa tried to ask it coolly, but her voice quivered, betraying the rage and the fear metastasizing inside of her.

"I'm going to shoot him too."

All the strength left her.

Theresa climbed onto her knees and tried to shield Ben with her body.

"Oh please," Pam said. "All I have to do . . ." She moved. Her voice moved. "Is stand up and walk over to *this* side of the cell. Then I have a clear shot again."

"Why are you doing this? You're my shrink."

"I was never your shrink."

"What are you talking about?"

"It's truly a shame, Theresa. I liked you. I enjoyed our sessions together. I want you to know that what's getting ready to happen to you and your son isn't personal. You just have the misfortune of being married to the man who destroyed this town."

"Ethan didn't destroy anything. He just told everyone the truth."

"That wasn't his place. The truth can be a dangerous thing for the weak-minded."

"You knew, didn't you?" Theresa asked. "All this time you knew."

"What? The truth about Wayward Pines? Of course I knew. I helped build this town, Theresa. I was here from the beginning. Day one. This place is the only home I ever had, and your husband ruined it. He ruined everything."

"Ethan didn't open the gate. He didn't turn off the fence and let all these monsters inside. Your boss did that."

"My boss, David Pilcher, created this town. Every house. Every road. He handpicked each resident. Each team member. Without him, you'd have been dead for centuries. How dare you question the man who gave you this life."

"Pam, please. My son isn't responsible for any of this. You know that."

"You don't understand, honey. This isn't about holding you and Ben responsible for Ethan's actions. We're way past that."

"Then what is it you want?" Theresa could feel tears coming, panic descending.

Ben was already crying, shaking in her arms.

"All I care about at this point is causing your husband pain. Nothing more," Pam said. "If he's still alive, he'll eventually come here looking for you, and do you know what he'll find?"

"You don't have to do this, Pam."

"The two of you dead and me sitting here. Waiting. I want him to know I did this before I kill him."

"Just listen—"

"I am listening. But before you start talking, ask yourself if you really believe you're going to change my mind."

Down the hall, somewhere in the lobby, Theresa heard the faintest sound.

Like a shard of glass splintering.

Thinking, *Please be an abby. Please.*

"Most of this town was killed last night," Theresa said. "I don't know how many of us are even left."

Another piece of glass crunched.

Theresa raised her voice a notch.

"But no matter how you feel toward my husband, how can you think that killing two of us who happened to survive is what's best for our species? We're on the verge of extinction!"

"Wow, that's a great point, Theresa. I hadn't thought of that."

"Really?"

"No, I'm just kidding. I don't give a shit." Pam racked a shell into the tube. "I promise I won't make you suffer. And honestly? Take a second to look on the bright side. At least you two didn't die at the hands of an abby. This way, you won't feel a thing. Well, you'll probably feel something, but it'll all be over before you know it."

"He's a child!" Theresa cried.

"Oh, would you mind sliding me the key to the cell before—"

The muzzle flash brightened the entire room.

The sound was deafening.

Theresa thinking, *We're dead. She did it.*

But she could still think.

She could still feel her son in her arms.

She braced for the pain to hit, but it didn't come.

Someone was saying her name, and over the ringing in her ears, it sounded as if the shouts were coming from the bottom of a deep hole.

Something sparked, a point of light flaring in her field of vision, Theresa wondering, *Is that the light at the end of the tunnel? Am I dead now, accelerating toward it? Is my son with me?*

It sparked again, only this time the light didn't die.

It grew brighter and brighter until a single flame ignited a tiny bundle of dried-out moss.

It was smoking now, and she could smell the smoke as she watched hands lift the burning tinder off the floor. The flames illuminated the dirtiest face she'd ever seen, engulfed by a shaggy beard that must have taken years to grow.

But those eyes . . .

Even in the diminishing firelight and through all the filth and the wildness in that face, she knew them. And not even the shock of almost dying could rival the shock of actually seeing them again.

The man said in a raspy voice, "Theresa! My love!"

Theresa released Ben and lunged forward.

As the light extinguished, she reached the bars and thrust her hands between them. She grabbed him, pulled him into the bars.

Adam Hassler reeked like a man who had been in the wilderness for years, and as her hands slid inside his duster and wrapped around his waist, she could feel that he was skin and bones.

"Adam?"

"It's me, Theresa."

"Oh my God!"

"I can't believe I'm actually touching you."

He kissed her through the bars.

As Ben climbed off the bed and approached, he said, "I thought you were dead."

"I should be dead, little man. I should've died a thousand times over."

ETHAN

He stood on the hood of Maggie's Jeep, staring out at the hundred fifty faces that had gathered around him in the ark. It felt strange to look at this entire group, which for fourteen years had worked together to keep its fellow human beings, the residents of Wayward Pines, living in the dark.

Ethan said, "Last night, I made a difficult choice. I told the residents of Wayward Pines the truth. I told them what year it was. I showed them an abby."

A voice in the midst of the crowd shouted, "You had no right!"

Ethan ignored this.

"I'm guessing none of you agree with that decision, and that's not really much of a surprise to me. But let's see if you agree with the decision David Pilcher made in response. He killed the power to the fence and opened the gate. At least five hundred abbies entered the valley in the middle of the night. More than half the town has been slaughtered. Those who managed to escape are stranded without food or water, and with no heat since Pilcher also cut off the power to the town."

Disbelief spread quickly across the faces.

Someone yelled, "Liar!"

"I understand that at some point in your lives before, each of you bought in hard to what David Pilcher was selling. And to be honest, he's a brilliant man. No one can deny that. No one can say he isn't a man of vision, and possibly the most ambitious person who ever lived. I understand what attracted you to him. It's a rush to keep company with someone who wields such power. Makes you feel better about yourself.

"From what I gather, a lot of you were at low points when David Pilcher came into your lives. He gave you purpose and meaning, and I totally get that. But he's as much of a monster as the abbies who lived beyond the fence. Maybe even more. The idea of Wayward Pines was always more important to him than the people who called that town home, and I'm sorry to say, it was more important than any of you.

"You all knew Alyssa. Everything I've heard confirms that she was universally loved inside this mountain. She didn't see eye to eye with her father. She believed the people of Wayward Pines deserved better than 24-7 surveillance, than being forced to murder one another, than never knowing the truth. What I'm about to show you is upsetting, and I apologize for that, but you need to know what kind of a man you served so you can begin to move past it."

Ethan pointed behind the crowd at a hundred-

273

inch monitor mounted to the rock beside the glass doors.

Most days, it displayed work schedules. Who was on shift in surveillance, security, and suspension. Arrival and departure times for transportation going back and forth to Wayward Pines. An in-mountain message system for Pilcher's inner circle.

Tonight, it would show David Pilcher, the creator of Wayward Pines, murdering his only daughter.

Ethan shouted to one of Ted's surveillance techs standing beneath the screen, "Play it!"

THERESA

The smoke trailed up and vented outside through the barred window near the ceiling. Flames ate away at the legs of Belinda's desk chair, fueled by a ream of printer paper. Ben sprawled on the single mattress, which Theresa had pulled off the metal frame and set next to the fire. She sat across from Hassler, holding her hands close to the heat.

On the other side of the bars, Pam's body lay slumped across the concrete, the pool of blood still expanding around her head.

"I saw the fence was down," Hassler said. "I came racing into town. I went to our house, but you weren't there. I looked everywhere. I thought you and Ben were dead. As I was looking for ammo in the sheriff's station, I heard your voice, begging Pam to spare you. Isn't exactly the homecoming I imagined."

"I didn't imagine one at all," Theresa said. "I was told you weren't coming back."

"What happened here?"

"The town knows the truth now."

"Everything?"

"Everything. We lost a lot of people. I guess the man who built all of this decided to trash his play set and go home."

"Who told everyone the truth?"

"There was a fête called for Kate and Harold Ballinger, but instead of executing them, the sheriff used the opportunity to lift the curtain."

"Pope?"

"Pope's dead, Adam." Theresa hesitated. "A lot has happened since you've been gone. Ethan is the sheriff now."

"Ethan's *here?*"

"He was introduced into the town a month or so ago. He turned this place upside down. Nothing's been the same since."

Hassler stared into the flames. "I didn't know he was here," he said.

"Why would you?"

"No, I just . . . Does Ethan know?"

"About us?"

"Yeah."

"No, I haven't told him. I mean, I was going to eventually, but Ben and I talked about it, decided there was no rush. We didn't think we'd ever see you again."

Tears dropped out of the corners of Hassler's eyes, carving clean trails through the grime embedded in his face.

Ben watched him from the mattress.

"It's like a nightmare," Hassler said.

"What?"

"Coming home to this. Every day I was out beyond the fence, facing death and hunger and thirst, it was you, only you, that kept me going. The thought of how our life would be when I got back."

"Adam."

"That year we lived together—"

"Please."

"Was the happiest I'd ever been. I love you. I never stopped." Hassler crawled around the bed of coals and put his arm around her. He looked at Ben. "I was a father to you, wasn't I?" He looked at Theresa. "And I was your man. Your protector."

"I wouldn't have survived Wayward Pines without you, Adam, but I thought you were never coming back. And then, suddenly, out of nowhere, my husband is here."

Somewhere outside, an abby howled.

Hassler pulled his backpack over, opened it, dug around inside until he emerged with a leather-bound journal. Tearing off the plastic, he opened the weathered book to the first page. In the firelight, he pointed to the inscription: *When you come back—and you will come back— I'm gonna fuck you, soldier, like you just came home from war.*

It broke her to see those words.

Knocked her flat.

She'd written them just before Hassler had left.

"I read it every day," he said. "You have no idea the hard times it got me through."

She couldn't see anything now, the tears

flowing, the emotion unfurling inside of her like a hemorrhage—too fast to staunch.

"I'm not asking you to predict the future," he said. "I'm talking about right now. This moment. Do you still love me, Theresa?"

She looked up at the matted beard, the scarred face, his hollowed-out eyes.

God, but she did.

"I never stopped," she whispered.

The relief in his eyes was like a stay of execution.

"I need to know something," she said. "When we were living together, did you know?"

"Did I know what?"

"About this town. What it was. All the secrets that were kept."

He stared into her eyes and said, "Until the day David Pilcher came to me and said I'd been chosen for a nomad mission beyond the fence, I only knew what you knew."

"Why did he send you out there?"

"To explore. To search for signs of human life outside our valley."

"Did you find any?"

"My last entry out there . . ." Hassler flipped to the end of his journal. "I wrote, 'I alone have the key to what will save us all. I'm literally the one man in the world who can save the world.' "

"So what is it?" Theresa asked. "What's the key?"

"To make our peace."

"With what?"

"With the fact that this is truly the end. The world belongs to the abbies now."

Even through her grief and shock, this statement registered.

Theresa felt suddenly, completely, alone.

"There isn't going to be some discovery that saves us," Hassler said. "That puts us back on the top of the food chain. This valley is the only place where we can survive. We're going to become extinct. That's simply a fact. Might as well do it with grace. Savor each day, each moment."

MUSTIN

Mustin brushed the snow off the rocks and settled down into his perch. Due to the sheer quantity of ammo he'd brought along this time, it had taken him an extra hour to reach the peak.

He'd scoped the town before, but of course he'd never had a target in the valley.

He zeroed out the scope on what was left of Sheriff Burke's Bronco.

It took him three shots, followed by three minor adjustments to the parallax, before he put a round exactly where he wanted it—through the front tire on the driver side.

The town had been laid out in regular blocks, three hundred feet long on each side, which meant that further adjustments would be simple now that he had his point of reference.

He cracked his neck.

Grabbing the bolt, he opened the breach and jacked the first round out of the five-capacity magazine.

Settling in behind the focus, he enabled his headset as he glassed Main Street.

"Mustin here, in position. Over."

Ethan Burke responded, "We're at the tunnel door. Over."

"Copy that. Beginning my first pass now. Stand by. Out."

There were bodies scattered up and down Main.

Five abbies feeding in the middle of the street in front of the Steaming Bean.

For now, he ignored the forest and the cliffs surrounding the town and took his time studying the east-west-running avenues, the north-south-running streets.

He scribbled a notation on his pad after every sighting.

Eleven minutes later, he tapped the TALK button on his headset.

"Mustin back. Over."

"Go ahead," Ethan said.

"I've got a visual on a hundred and five aberrations. About half of them are moving in groups of between fifteen and twenty. The others are ranging solo through town. No sign of survivors yet."

Ethan said, "You've got twenty minutes and then we're rolling in. Over."

Mustin smiled. A deadline. He liked that.

He asked, "We taking bets? Over."

"What are you talking about?"

"Number of kills. Over."

"Just get to it."

Mustin started on the south end of Main and worked slowly north.

Fifteen hits.

Five misses.

Twelve kills.

Three left to wish they were dead, dragging themselves across the pavement.

He moved up to Seventh Street, made his adjustments, and went to work. Near the school, he sighted down a group of eighteen abbies sleeping in the street. He shot four of them before the others woke up and realized they were under attack. Brought down five more as they scattered.

It went on like this, and he had to admit it was the most fun he'd ever had with his AWM sniper rifle.

With five minutes remaining, he shot three abbies on the road south of town, killed two more in the vicinity of the gardens. As the sheriff's voice came back over the headset, he put a round through the head of an abby running at full speed past the hospital.

"Time's up," Ethan said. "Over."

"Forty-four," Mustin said. "Over."

"Excuse me?"

"There are forty-four less abbies to contend with. Over."

"Impressive. Is the fence holding?"

Mustin swung the rifle south, glassing the forest in the vicinity of the fence.

He reported, "The gate's still closed. Now I can give you some cover once you get into town, but shooting down into the forest is iffy at best. Over."

"Understood. You'll be our eyes. Kill what you can. Tell us what's coming. Over."

Mustin reloaded the magazine and chambered the next round.

He glassed what he could see of the woods and the boulders that surrounded the entrance to the superstructure.

"You're clear to roll out," he said.

ETHAN

He rode in the front passenger seat of an armored Humvee, with Alan behind the wheel.

In his side mirror, he could see the metalworkers welding shut the entrance to the superstructure.

Up on the roof of the Humvee, one of the guards manned a .50 cal machine gun.

There were two Dodge Ram pickup trucks behind them, two men standing in the back of the first with pump-action shotguns.

The second Ram carried the chain gun.

Two transfer trucks followed the Rams, and a third pickup truck brought up the rear holding six guards in the bed, all armed to the teeth.

In Ethan's headset, Mustin said, "I'd advise staying off Main. What's your route? Over."

Alan turned out of the woods and onto the road into town.

"Thirteenth to Fifth," Ethan said, "then three blocks to the school. Any company?"

"See that guy in the distance?"

Ethan squinted through the windshield.

A hundred yards up the road, an abby was squatting over the double yellow. The sound of approaching engines caught its attention, and as it stood, a puff of red mist exploded out of the side of its head.

"You got a few other stragglers in your path," Mustin said. "I'll start clearing the way. Over."

The sun had yet to rise above the cliffs, and the valley ahead was still draped in the light of early morning.

"Get any sleep?" Alan asked.

"What do you think?"

KATE

She heard the tat-tat-tat of automatic gunfire.

Everyone in the classroom did.

She and Spitz went to work dragging the furniture away from the door and pulling the nails out of the frame.

They got it open, told everyone to wait.

Rushed out into the hall.

Up the stairs.

The noise of gunfire growing louder, and in the space between shots another sound becoming audible—the rumble of engines.

At the exit, Kate raised her AR-15 and told Spitz to get the door.

He pulled it open.

She took two steps through the threshold.

There were abbies in the schoolyard running toward a convoy of vehicles in the intersection of Tenth and Fifth—a Humvee, three pickup trucks, and two eighteen-wheelers.

An abby broke off from the pack and came hurtling toward her.

Spitz said, "You got him?"

She let it get closer, within twenty feet.

"Kate?"

She squeezed—put three bursts in a nice pattern

through its chest and dropped it five feet from the door.

Now came a noise like thunder, and with it, from the second pickup truck, a bright orange muzzle flash from a gun so big it should've been mounted on an attack helicopter.

It cut an entire row of abbies in half.

The front passenger door of the Humvee swung open.

When Ethan stepped out, her heart swelled.

She watched him come around the front of the vehicle and run toward the fence.

As he climbed over, four abbies charged him from the playground.

Kate took aim and ripped through the rest of her magazine, bringing them all down.

Ethan looked over, eyebrows up in surprise.

For a moment, the shooting had stopped.

There were abbies lying everywhere and men climbing down out of the truck beds, beginning to set up a perimeter.

Kate ran toward him, Ethan limping, carrying a shotgun, his jeans ripped all to hell, his shirt in tatters, face streaked with blood.

Tears blurred her vision and she wiped them away.

They reached each other and she threw her arms around him.

"How are the injured?" he asked.

"One died. One's hanging on. Barely."

"I brought trucks. We're taking everyone out of here, into the mountain."

"Have you found Harold?"

"Not yet."

"What about Theresa and Ben?"

He shook his head.

Tears were running down her face and her eyes were shut tight and Ethan kept saying her name, kept saying that everything would be okay, but she couldn't stop crying and she wouldn't let him go.

ETHAN

As he held Kate, he glimpsed a man walking down Tenth Street in a long, black duster that fell to his ankles, his face hidden under a black cowboy hat and a long, unkempt beard.

Ethan said, "Who the hell is that?"

Kate turned her head. "I've never seen him before."

Ethan started across the schoolyard, scaled the fence, and moved out into the middle of the street.

The man in black carried a Winchester rifle, which rested against his shoulder, and his shuffling gait scraped his boots across the pavement. He stopped several feet away from Ethan—a haggard, vile-smelling specimen. He would've looked like a homeless eccentric were it not for his eyes. No insanity there. Just clear, lucid intensity.

The man said, "Well goddamn, Ethan."

"I'm sorry, do we know each other?"

Ethan just glimpsed the man's smile through the shambles of his beard.

"Do we know each other?" the man laughed, his voice scratchy, like his larynx had been wrapped in sandpaper. "I'll give you a hint. Last time we spoke, I sent you here."

Recognition fired in Ethan's brain.

Synapses connecting the dots.

He cocked his head and said, "Adam?"

"So what I hear, you started this mess."

"You've been in town all this time?"

"No, no. I just got back."

"Back from where?"

"Out there. Beyond."

"You're a nomad?"

"I've been gone three and a half years. Came back through the fence yesterday at dawn."

"Adam—"

"I know you have questions, but if you're looking for your family, I found them last night."

"Where?"

"Theresa had locked herself and Ben into the jail cell in the sheriff's station."

"They're there right now?"

"Yes, and—"

Ethan took off running up Tenth Street, maintained a full sprint for six blocks until he rushed into the sheriff's station, gasping for breath.

"Theresa!" he shouted.

"Ethan?"

He shot down the hallway toward the cell at the north end of the building, and when he saw his wife and son alive behind the bars, his eyes filled with tears.

Theresa fumbled with the key, turned the lock.

Ethan pushed the door open and embraced her, kissing her face, her hands, like it was the first time he'd ever touched her.

"I thought I'd lost you," he said.

"You almost did."

Ben nearly tackled him.

"You okay, buddy?"

"Yeah, Dad, but we almost died."

Gunshots started up again, several blocks away.

"You brought the cavalry," Theresa said.

"I did."

"Have you rescued a lot of people?"

"There's a group in the basement of the school that's going to be okay. A security team is fanning out through town right now, killing everything that isn't human, saving whoever else they can. Why didn't you and Ben stay in the cavern?"

"The abbies came back," Ben said. "A lot of people stayed, but Mom and I found another way down the cliffs."

"Those who stayed, I don't think they made it," Theresa said.

Through the bars, Ethan noticed Pam, dead on the floor. "She found us here last night," Theresa said. "We were locked in the cell, with no weapons. She was going to kill us."

"Why?"

"To hurt you." Theresa seemed to shudder at the memory of it. "Adam Hassler saved us," she said.

"Did you know he was here?" Ethan asked.

"No."

The chain gun started up again.

Ethan pulled out his radio, and said, "Burke here. Over."

Alan's voice responded: "Yeah, go ahead? Over."

"Can you send a truck up to the sheriff's station? I found my family. I want to get them someplace safe."

THERESA

WAYWARD PINES
FIVE YEARS AGO

She stands in the rain, barefoot, her hospital gown soaked straight through to her skin, staring up at a twenty-five-foot fence whose barbed wires crackle with electricity.

Two signs nearby warn:

HIGH VOLTAGE
RISK OF DEATH

And:

RETURN TO WAYWARD PINES
BEYOND THIS POINT YOU WILL DIE

She crumples down in the dirt.
Cold.
Shivering.
It's dusk, on the verge of becoming too dark to see in these woods.
She's at the end. At her end.
No one to turn to.

Nowhere left to run.

She crashes.

Hard.

Sobbing uncontrollably as the freezing rain beats down on her.

Hands grab her by the shoulders.

She reacts like a wounded animal, tearing herself away and scrambling off on all fours as a voice calls after her, "Theresa!"

But she doesn't stop.

Struggling up onto her feet, she digs in for a sprint, feet sliding in the wet pine needles.

The hands tackle her to the ground, her face crushed into mud, pressing down on top of her and trying to roll her over. She fights back with everything she has, arms tucked into her sides, thinking, If those hands get anywhere near my mouth, this asshole is going to lose fingers.

But he manages to roll her onto her back and hold her arms down, pinning her legs under his knees.

"Let go!" she screams.

"Stop fighting."

That voice.

She looks up at her attacker. It's almost too dark to see now, but she recognizes his face.

From another life.

A better time.

She stops struggling.

"Adam?"

"It's me."

He releases her arms and helps her to sit up.

"What are you . . . ? Why . . . ?" So many questions screaming through her mind she can't focus on which one to give voice to. At last she lands on, "What's happening to me?"

"You're in Wayward Pines, Idaho."

"I know that. Why is there no road out of here? Why is there a fence? Why won't anyone tell me what's happening?"

"I know you have questions—"

"Where's my son?"

"I may be able to help you find Ben."

"You know where he is?"

"No, but I—"

"Where is he?" she screams. "I have to—"

"Theresa, you're endangering yourself right now. You're putting both of our lives at risk. I want you to come with me."

"Where?"

"To my house."

"Your house?"

He takes off his rain jacket, wraps it around her shoulders, and pulls her up onto her feet.

"Why do you have a house here, Adam?"

"Because I live here."

"For how long?"

"A year and a half."

"That's impossible."

"I know it must feel that way to you right now. I'm sure everything seems strange and wrong in this moment. Where are your shoes?"

"I don't know."

"I'm going to carry you."

Hassler scoops her up into his arms like she weighs nothing.

Theresa looks into his face, and despite the horror of her last five days here, she can't deny the comfort she feels staring into familiar eyes.

"Why are you here, Adam?"

"I know you have a lot of questions. Let me just get you home first, okay? You're practically hypothermic."

"Have I lost my mind? I don't know anything anymore. I woke up in the hospital here, and these last few days have been—"

"Look at me. You're not crazy, Theresa."

"Then what?"

"You're just in a different kind of place now."

298

"I don't know what that means."

"I know, but if you trust me, I swear I'll take care of you. I'll make sure nothing happens to you. And I'll help you find your son."

Despite the new protection of his jacket, she trembles violently in Hassler's arms.

He carries her through the dark forest and the pouring rain.

Her last memory before waking in this town is of sitting in her home in Queen Anne across from a man named David Pilcher. It was the night she'd thrown a party to celebrate her missing husband's life, and after all the guests had left, Pilcher had shown up on her doorstep in the wee hours with a mysterious offer: come with him, and she and Ben could be reunited with Ethan.

Apparently, the promise had not been kept.

Theresa lies on a sofa pulled close to an open woodstove, watching as Adam Hassler adds pine logs to the fire. The deep-down cold is beginning to retreat from her bones. She hasn't slept in forty-eight hours—since waking up for a second time in a hospital bed to that awful, smiling nurse—but now she can feel sleep stalking her. She won't be able to hold out much longer.

Hassler stokes the flames up into a roaring blaze, the sap boiling and popping inside the wood.

Every light in the living room is out.

Firelight colors the walls.

She can hear the steady rain hammering the tin roof above her head, ready to put her under.

Hassler scoots back from the fire, sits on the sofa's edge.

He looks down at her with a kindness in his eyes that she hasn't seen in days.

"Is there anything I can get for you?" he asks. "Water? More blankets?"

"I'm okay. Well, not okay, but . . ."

He smiles. "I know what you mean."

She stares up at him. "These have been the weirdest, worst days of my life."

"I know."

"What's happening to me?"

"I can't explain it to you."

"Can't or won't?"

"You disappeared from Seattle the night of Ethan's celebration-of-life party. You and Ben."

"Right."

"I figured you had gone to Wayward

Pines looking for Ethan, so I went looking for you."

"Shit. You're here because of me."

"I drove into town two days before Christmas. All I remember is a Mack truck coming out of nowhere, sideswiping my car. I woke up in the hospital, just like you did. No phone, no wallet. Have you tried to call out to Seattle?"

"I phoned my sister, Darla, I don't know how many times from that pay phone beside the bank, but it's always either a wrong number or there's no dial tone."

"Same thing happened to me."

"So how do you have a house here now?"

"I have a job too."

"What?"

"You're looking at the sous-chef in training at the Aspen House, nicest restaurant in Wayward Pines."

Theresa searches his face for signs of bullshit, but he looks absolutely sincere.

She says, "You're the special agent in charge of the Secret Service field office in Seattle. You—"

"Things have changed."

"Adam—"

"Just listen to me." He puts his hand on her shoulder. She can feel its weight through the blanket. "All the questions, all the fears you have, I had them too. I still have them. That doesn't change. But there are no answers to be had in this valley. There's only a right way to live and all the other ways that get you killed. As your friend, Theresa, I hope you can hear me. If you don't stop running, this town will murder you."

She looks away from Hassler, into the flames.

The firelight blurring through a sheet of tears.

The scary thing, the truly scary thing, is that she believes him.

One hundred percent. There's something wrong, something evil about this place.

"I feel so lost," she says.

"I know." He squeezes her shoulder. "I've been there, and I'm going to help you in every way I possibly can."

ETHAN

He found Kate that evening, sitting in her living room, staring into the cold, dark fireplace.

He sat down beside her, set his shotgun on the hardwood floor.

Abbies had broken in at some point. The front windows were smashed out, the interior looked vandalized, and it still smelled like those creatures—a harsh, alien stench.

"What are you doing in here?" Ethan asked.

Kate shrugged. "I guess I feel like if I wait here long enough, he'll come walking through that door."

Ethan put his arm around her.

She said, "But he's not going to walk through that door ever again, is he?"

It seemed as if it was only by sheer force of will that she held the tears back.

Ethan shook his head.

"Because you found him."

The light splintering through the busted windows was growing weaker by the moment. Soon, it would be dark in the valley.

"His group was run down in one of the tunnels," Ethan said.

Still no tears came.

She just breathed in and out.

"I want to see him," she said.

"Of course. We've been gathering up the dead all day, doing what we can to prepare them for—"

"I'm not afraid to see him torn up, Ethan. I just want to see him."

"Okay."

"How many did we lose?"

"We're still recovering bodies, so right now we're only counting survivors. Out of four hundred sixty-one in-town residents, we're down to a hundred and eight. Seventy-five are still unaccounted for."

"I'm glad it was you who came with this news," she said.

"They're bringing all the survivors into the mountain for the next few nights."

"I'm staying right here."

"It's not safe, Kate. There are still abbies in the valley. We haven't gotten them all. There's no power. No heat. When the sun drops, it's going to get very dark and very cold. The abbies still inside the fence will come back into town."

She looked at him. She said, "I don't care."

"You want me to sit with you for a while?"

"I want to be alone."

Ethan rose to his feet, every inch of his body sore, bruised, done. "I'll leave this shotgun with you," he said, "just in case."

He couldn't be sure that she'd heard him.

She was utterly elsewhere.

"Is your family safe?" Kate asked.

"They are."

She nodded.

"I'll come back in the morning," he said. "Take you to see Harold." He moved toward the front door.

Kate said, "Hey."

He looked back.

"This isn't your fault."

That night, Ethan lay next to Theresa in a warm, dark room, deep inside the superstructure.

Ben slept on a rollaway at the foot of their bed, the boy snoring quietly.

The nightlight across the room put out a soft blue and Ethan stared into the glow. The first night in ages he could actually sleep in warmth, in safety, without a camera spying on him. Sleep was there for the taking, but he couldn't find his way in.

Theresa's hand moved around his side and across his stomach.

She whispered, "You awake?"

He rolled over to face her, and by the illumination of the nightlight, saw the glistening in her eyes, the wetness on her face.

"I need to tell you something," she said.

"Okay."

"You've only been back in our lives for barely a month."

"Right."

"We'd already been here for five years. We didn't know where we were. If we were."

"I already know all this."

"What I'm trying to say is . . . there was someone before you came."

"Someone," Ethan said, a sudden pressure building in his chest, a weight pressing down on his lungs, stopping him from drawing a full breath.

"I thought you were dead. Or that maybe I was."

"Who?"

"When I first came to town, I didn't know a soul. I woke up here just like you did, and Ben wasn't with me, and—"

"Who?"

"You saw that Adam Hassler is here."

"Hassler?"

"He saved my life, Ethan. He helped me find Ben."

"Are you for real?"

She was crying now. "I lived with him in that house on Sixth Street for over a year, up until the day he was sent away."

"You were *with* Hassler?"

A sob caught in her throat. "I thought you were dead. You know how this town can mess with you."

"Did you share his bed?"

"Ethan—"

"Did you?"

She nodded.

He rolled away from her onto his back and stared at the ceiling. No idea how to even *begin* to process this. All he had were questions, images of Hassler and his wife, and a raw, combustive pool of confusion, anger, and fear coalescing deep inside of him that was accelerating toward supernova.

"Talk to me," she said. "Don't shut down."

"Were you in love with him?"

"Yes."

"Are you still?"

"I'm confused."

"That's not a no."

"Do you want me to protect your feelings, Ethan, or do you want me to be honest?"

"Why didn't you tell me?"

"Because I wasn't prepared to have this conversation. You'd only been here a month. We were just starting to reconnect again."

"You never were. Your lover showed up out of nowhere and forced your hand."

"That is not true, Ethan. I swear I would've told you. I was assured that Adam was never coming back. And by the way? I was with Hassler when I thought you were dead. You fucked Kate Hewson while I was still very much alive. While I was your wife. So let's keep this shit in perspective, shall we?"

"Do you want to be with him?"

"If he hadn't found me, I would've kept running and running until they murdered me. There is no doubt in my mind. He supported me, he took care of me when there was no one else to do it. When you weren't around."

Ethan turned back onto his side and faced his wife, their noses touching, her breath in his face and a roiling mass of emotion inside of him that he wasn't completely certain he could keep tied down.

"Do you want to be with him?" he asked again.

"I don't know."

"You don't *know?* Does that mean maybe?"

"I have never been loved the way that man loves me." Ethan stopped breathing. "If this is hard for you to hear, I'm sorry, but I was his world, Ethan, and it . . ." She let the words go, let them trail off into nothing.

"What?"

"I shouldn't say any—"

"No, finish your thought."

"It was like nothing I'd ever experienced. Since the first time you and I met, I have loved you with everything I have. Can I just be straight up with you? I have always loved you more than you loved me."

"That is not true."

"You know it is. My loyalty, my devotion to you has been total. If our marriage was a rope, you on one end, me on the other, I was always pulling a little bit harder. And sometimes a lot."

"This is punishment, isn't it? For Kate."

"Not everything is about you. This is about me and this man I fell in love with while you were gone, and who's now back, and I have no fucking idea how to handle it. Can you put yourself in my shoes for two seconds?"

Ethan sat up in bed, threw back the covers.

"Don't leave," she said.

"I just need some air."

"I shouldn't have told you."

"No, you should've told me on day one."

He climbed out of bed, walked out of their room wearing socks, pajama bottoms, and a wifebeater.

It was two or three in the morning, and Level 4 stood empty, the fluorescent lights humming quietly overhead.

Ethan walked down the corridor. Behind every door he passed, residents of Wayward Pines slept safe and sound. There was comfort in knowing that some had been saved.

The cafeteria was closed, dark.

Stopping at the doors to the gymnasium, he peered through the glass. In the low light, he saw the raised basketball hoops, the court covered in cots. The people in the mountain had volunteered as a group to give up their rooms on Level 4 to the refugees, a gesture he hoped would be a good omen for the tough transition to come.

Down on Level 2, he swiped his card and stepped into surveillance.

Alan sat at the console, watching the screens.

He looked back as Ethan entered, and said, "You're up late."

Ethan took a seat beside him.

"Anything?" he asked.

"I disabled the motion sensors that powered up the cameras, so they're running all the time now. I'm sure the batteries won't last much longer. I've spotted a few dozen abbies back in town. I'll take a team down in the morning first thing to finish them off."

"And the fence?"

"Full power. All levels in the green. You should really get some sleep."

"I don't see a lot of that in my future."

Alan laughed. "Tell me about it."

"Thank you, by the way," Ethan said. "If you hadn't backed me up yesterday—"

"You honored my friend."

"The people from town—"

"Don't let this out, but we call them townies."

Ethan said, "They're going to be looking to me. I have a feeling the people in the mountain will be looking to you."

"Looks that way. There are going to be some

tough choices to make in our future, and a right way and a wrong way to handle them."

"What do you mean?"

"Pilcher ran things a certain way."

"Yeah. *His*."

"I'm not defending the man, but sometimes situations arise that are so pivotal, so life and death, one or two strong people need to call the shots."

"Think Pilcher has any diehards in the mountain?" Ethan asked.

"What do you mean? True believers?"

"Exactly."

"Everyone in this mountain is a true believer. Don't you understand what we gave up to be here?"

"No."

"Everything. We believed that man when he said the old world was dying and that we had a chance to be a part of the new world to come. I sold my house, my cars, cashed out my 401(k), left my family. I gave him everything I had."

"Can I ask you something?"

"Sure."

"You might have missed it with all the other excitement, but we had a nomad return today."

"Yeah, Adam Hassler."

"So you know him."

"Not well. I'm shocked he made it back."

311

"I'd like to know more about him. Was he a townie before he left on his mission?"

"I couldn't tell you. You should go talk to Francis Leven."

"Who's that?"

"The steward of the superstructure."

"Which means . . ."

"He tracks supplies, system integrity, the status of people in suspension and out. He's a wealth of institutional memory. The heads of each group report to him, and he reports, well, reported, to Pilcher."

"Never met him."

"He's a recluse. Keeps mostly to himself."

"Where would I find him?"

"His office is tucked way back in the ark."

Ethan stood.

The pain meds were fading.

The wear and tear of the last forty-eight hours becoming suddenly pronounced.

As Ethan started toward the door, Alan said, "One last thing."

"Yeah?"

"We finally found Ted. He was in his room, stuffed in his closet, stabbed to death. Pilcher had cut his microchip out and destroyed it."

Ethan would've thought that, after a day like this, one more piece of shitty news would crash into his psyche like a wave against a seawall, but it penetrated. Deeply.

He left Alan and went back out into the corridor, started up the steps toward the Level 4 dormitories, but then stopped.

Turning back, he descended the last flight of stairs to the first level.

Margaret, the abby whose intelligence Pilcher had been testing for the last few months, was up, pacing in her cage under the glare of the fluorescents.

Ethan put his face to the small window and stared through, his breath fogging the glass.

Last time he'd seen this abby, she'd been sitting peacefully in the corner.

Docile. Humanlike.

Now she looked agitated. Not angry, not vicious. Just nervous.

Because so many of your brothers and sisters have come into our valley? Ethan wondered. *Because so many have been killed, even in this complex?* Pilcher had told him that the abbies communicated through pheromones. Used them like words, he'd said.

Margaret saw Ethan.

She crept on all fours over toward the door and stood on her hind legs.

Ethan's eyes and the abby's eyes were just inches away, separated by the glass.

Up close, hers were almost pretty.

Ethan moved deeper into the corridor.

Six doors down, he looked through the window of another cage.

There was no bed, no chair.

Just floor and walls and David Pilcher sitting in a corner, his head hung as if he'd fallen asleep sitting up. The lights burned down through the window and lit the left side of the man's face.

He hadn't been allowed to keep any personal effects, including a razor, and white stubble was beginning to overspread his jaw.

You did this, Ethan thought. *You ruined so many lives. My life. My marriage.*

If he'd had a keycard to this cell, Ethan would've rushed inside and beat the man to death.

Everyone—townies and mountain people—came down for the burials.

The cemetery was too full to accommodate all the bodies so an open field on the southern border of the graveyard was annexed.

Ethan helped Kate with Harold.

The sky was gray.

No one spoke.

Tiny flakes of snow swirled through the crowd.

There was just the constant sound of shovels stabbing into the cold, hard ground.

As the digging finished, people crumpled down in the snow-frosted grass beside loved ones, or what was left of them, the dead wrapped tightly in once-white sheets. The digging had given them something to do, but as they sat motionless and cold beside lost fathers, mothers, brothers, sisters, husbands, wives, friends, and children, muffled sobs began to rise up from the crowd.

Ethan walked out into the middle of the field.

From where he stood, it was a crushing collection of sights and sounds: all those little mounds of dirt, the dead waiting to be lowered into their final resting places, the grieving of those who had lost everything, the mountain people standing behind the townies looking solemnly on, and the column of smoke at the north end of town coughing spirals of sweet-smelling black into the sky as six hundred abby corpses smoldered into nothing.

Except for David Pilcher, the man responsible for all this pain, every human being left on earth was in this field.

Even Adam Hassler, standing on the outskirts with Theresa and Ben.

Ethan was struck with a single, terrifying thought: *I'm losing my wife.*

He made a slow turn, studying all the faces. The grief was overpowering. A living thing.

"I don't know what to say. Words can't make any of this feel better. We lost three-quarters of our people, and it's going to be hard for a long, long time. Let's do what we can to help one another, because it's just us out here alone in the world."

As everyone began to lift the bodies gently down into their graves, Ethan headed back across the field, through the falling snow toward Kate.

He helped her lower Harold into his grave.

Then they took up their shovels, and, along with everyone else, began to fill in the dirt.

THERESA

She walked with Hassler through the forest south of town, snowflakes drifting down between the pines. Adam had shaved his beard and cut his hair, but the smooth skin only underscored the gaunt, drawn quality of his face. He looked emaciated. Like a refugee of a starving world. She couldn't get past how surreal it felt to be physically close to him again. Before she'd given him up for dead, she'd made it a habit of imagining their reunion. None of those fantasies had been anything like the real thing.

"Are you sleeping all right?" Theresa asked.

"It's funny. You don't know how many nights out in the wild I dreamed of sleeping in a bed again. All the pillows, the covers, the warmth, the safety. Being able to reach out in the dark to a bedside table and wrap my hand around a cool glass of water. But since I've been back, I've barely slept. Guess I got used to sleeping in a bivy sack, tied into a tree thirty feet off the ground. How about you?"

"It's difficult," she said.

"Nightmares?"

"I keep dreaming that things went another way. That those abbies got into the jail cell."

"How's Ben?"

317

"He's okay. I can tell he's trying to wrap his head around what happened. A lot of his classmates didn't make it."

"He saw things no kid should ever have to see."

"He's twelve now. Can you believe it?"

"He looks so much like you, Theresa. I've wanted to see more of him, to just talk to him, but it didn't feel right. Not yet."

"That's probably best," she said.

"Where's Ethan?"

"He was going to stay with Kate for a while after the burial."

"Some things never change, huh?"

"She lost her husband. She doesn't really have anyone else." Theresa sighed. "I told Ethan."

"Told him . . ."

"About us."

"Oh."

"I didn't have a choice. I couldn't just go on keeping it from him."

"How'd he take it?"

"You know Ethan. How do you think?"

"But he understands what the situation was, right? That you and I were trapped here. That we thought he was dead."

"I explained everything."

"So does he not believe you?"

"I don't know if it's that so much as he's just trying to come to terms with the idea that, well, you know."

"That I was fucking his wife."

Theresa stopped.

So quiet in the woods.

"It was good, right?" Hassler asked. "When it was just you, me, and Ben. I made you happy, didn't I?"

"Very."

"You have no idea what I'd do for you, Theresa."

She looked up into his eyes.

He stared at her with such love.

An energy in the air, Theresa could sense that this moment carried more heft than she realized. Her heart had once been wide open to this man, and if she let him keep looking at her like this, like she was the only thing that existed in his world—

He moved in.

Kissed her.

At first, she drew back.

Then she let him.

Then she kissed back.

He walked her slowly back against a pine tree, and as he pressed into her she ran her fingers through his hair.

As he kissed her neck, she tilted her head back and looked up into snowflakes that fell and melted on her face, and then he was unzipping her jacket, his fingers making quick work of the buttons on her shirt underneath, and she found herself reaching for his.

She stopped.

"What?" he asked, breathless. "What's wrong?"

"I'm still married."

"That didn't stop him." There was a part of her that wanted him to talk her into it. To keep pushing. To *not* stop. "Remember how he made you feel? What was it you said to me, Theresa? Your love for him always burned at a hotter temperature."

"I've seen him change in the last month. I've seen glimmers of—"

"Glimmers? Is that all you felt from me? Glimmers?"

She shook her head.

"I love you with everything I have. Nothing held back. No bets hedged. All in. Every second of every day."

Off in the distance, a scream ripped through the forest.

An abby.

High-pitched. Delicate. Bloodcurdling.

Hassler staggered back from her, and she could see the intensity hardening across his brow.

"Is it—"

"I don't think it's inside the fence," he said.

"Let's get out of here anyway," she said.

She buttoned up, zipped up.

They started back toward town.

Her body was humming and her head was spinning.

They reached the road and walked down the double yellow line.

Buildings appeared in the distance.

In silence, they headed into Wayward Pines.

She felt reckless but she went on with him.

At the intersection of Sixth and Main, Hassler said, "Can we go see it together?"

"Sure."

They walked down the sidewalk of their neighborhood.

No one out.

The houses empty and dark.

Everything looked cold and gray and void of life.

"Doesn't smell like us in here anymore," he said as they stood at the foot of the stairs in what had once been their yellow Victorian.

He moved into the kitchen, through the dining room, and back out into the hallway.

"I can't imagine how difficult this is for you, Theresa."

"You have no idea."

Hassler emerged out of the shadow of the hall, and when he reached her he went down on one knee.

"I think this is how it's done, right?" he asked.

"What are you doing, Adam?"

He took her hand.

His were rough, not the hands she remembered. They'd become wiry and hard as steel, and there was dirt from beyond the fence embedded so deep underneath his fingernails she couldn't imagine it ever washing away.

"Be with me, Theresa, whatever that means in this new world we're living in."

Tears dripped off her chin onto the floor.

Her voice trembled.

She said, "I'm already—"

"I know you're married, I know Ethan's here, but I don't give a shit and you shouldn't either. Life is too hard and too short not to be with the one you love. So choose me."

ETHAN

Francis Leven lived in a stand-alone structure in a far corner of the ark, built into an overhang in the rock wall. Ethan's keycard didn't work on the reader, so he banged his fist against the steel door instead.

"Mr. Leven!"

After a moment, the lock retracted.

The door cracked open.

The man who answered stood barely five feet tall, and he was dressed in a bathrobe, which filth and time had degraded to something less than white. Forty-five or fifty, Ethan guessed, although Leven's advanced state of dishevelment made that approximation iffy. His dishwater hair was shoulder-length and shiny with grease, and through large blue eyes, he regarded Ethan with unveiled suspicion that bordered on malice.

"What do you want?" Leven asked.

"I need to talk to you."

"I'm busy. Another time."

Leven tried to shut the door, but Ethan shoved it open hard and forced his way inside.

Candy bar wrappers littered the floor and the air carried a moist, moldy scent, like the living space of a sixteen-year-old boy, but spiked with the caustic odor of stale coffee.

The sole illumination came from recessed lighting in the ceiling and the glow of the giant LED displays that covered almost every square foot of wall space. Ethan stared at the one closest to him, which showed a digital pie chart. At a glance, the chart appeared to reflect the atmospheric breakdown of the superstructure's air content.

He didn't know what to make of all the screens.

They showed a seemingly incomprehensible array of data.

—Sets of temperature gradients in Kelvin.

—A digital representation of what Ethan assumed were the one thousand suspension chambers.

—Vital stats on the two hundred fifty people still warm and breathing on the planet.

—Drone footage.

—A full biometric readout on the female abby in captivity.

It was like the surveillance center on steroids.

"I would like for you to leave," Leven said. "No one bothers me here."

"Pilcher's finished. In case you didn't get the memo, you work for me now."

"That's debatable."

"What is this place?"

Leven glared him down through a thick pair of glasses.

Stubborn. Resisting.

Ethan said, "I'm not leaving."

"I monitor the systems that keep the super-structure and Wayward Pines functioning. We call it mission control."

"Which systems?"

"All of them. Electrical. Hull. Filtration. Surveillance. Suspension. Ventilation. The reactor underneath us that powers everything."

Ethan moved deeper into the nerve center.

"And it's just you responsible for all of this?"

Leven let slip a smirk. "I have minions. You know, in the event I'm hit by the proverbial bus."

Ethan smiled, detecting the first inkling of a wicked sense of humor.

"I hear you keep to yourself," Ethan said.

"I'm in charge of the engine that makes our existence possible. I work eighteen hours a day, every day. Before the burial this morning, I hadn't seen the sky in three years."

"Doesn't sound like much of a life."

"Well, it's the one I have. I happen to love it."

Ethan approached a set of monitors in a dark alcove that streamed lines of code at the speed of a stock-market ticker.

"What's this?" Ethan asked.

"Beautiful, isn't it? I'm running some pro-jections."

"Projections on . . . ?"

Leven came and stood beside him. They

watched the lines of code spilling down the screens like a waterfall.

Leven said, finally, "The viability of what remains of our species. See, things were dire long before David had his little temper tantrum and threw his people to the wolves."

"Dire how?"

"Follow."

Leven showed Ethan over to the main console, where they sat down in oversize leather chairs facing an expansive array of screens.

"Before the massacre in the valley, there were a hundred sixty souls living in the mountain," Leven said. "Four hundred sixty-one living in Wayward Pines. Our data only goes back fourteen years, but the first killing freeze typically comes in late August. You haven't been here for a winter yet, but they're long and brutal. The snow can get ten, fifteen feet deep in the valley. There's no garden to harvest from. No fruit, no vegetables. We subsist solely on our reserve of freeze-dried meals, supplements, and meat rations. You want to hear a dirty little secret? Now that this is all on you? David Pilcher never intended for us to stay in this valley indefinitely."

"What are you talking about?"

"He miscalculated how uninhabitable and hostile this world would become."

Ethan felt something go dark inside of him.

"I'm rerunning my calculations," Leven said,

"but it's looking like our winter rations will run out in four point two years. Now, there are things we can do to delay the inevitable, like enforcing reduced rations. But that only buys us, at most, another year or two."

"Not to be callous, but don't we have less mouths to feed now?"

"Yes, but the abbies wiped out our cattle, our dairy. There will be no milk, no meat. It would take years to reboot the herd."

"Then we have to find a way to store what we grow for the winter."

"Our current setup in town doesn't produce enough food to feed us and save for the future."

"You mean we eat what we grow?"

"Exactly. And pretty much right away. We're just too far north. Two thousand years ago, we might have been able to make this growing season work, but it's gotten shorter and harsher. And these last few years have been the coldest yet. Here's what I wanted to show you."

Leven input some new code via the touch screen.

A list began to scroll.

Ethan examined the monitor above him.

Rice: 17%

Flour: 6%

Sugar: 11%

Grain: 3%

Iodized Salt: 32%

Corn: 0%
Vitamin C: 55%
Soybeans: 0%
Powdered Milk: 0%
Malt: 4%
Barley: 3%
Yeast: 1%

The list continued on.

Ethan said, "These are the reserve staple levels?"

"Yes. And as you can see, it's critical."

"What was Pilcher planning to do?"

"With our full in-town population, we might have had the manpower to expand our gardens fast enough to meet demand. We were also looking into building a network of greenhouses, but see the problem comes with snow loads in the winter. If enough weight were to build up on the glass roofs, they'd collapse. Again, we're just too far north."

"Do the people in the mountain understand what's coming?"

"No. David didn't want to spook anyone until we had come up with a solution."

"And you haven't."

"There isn't one," Leven said. "Five-year models confirm this valley will become uninhabitable. If we catch a really bad winter, possibly sooner. We're all from the modern age. If push came to shove, we might have been able to adopt an agrarian lifestyle in a more temperate climate. But with weather like this? The only lifestyle that might support us is the nomadic hunter-gatherer."

"Except we're trapped in this valley."

"Precisely."

"What about the abbies?" Ethan asked.

"As a food source?"

"Yeah."

"First off, gross. Secondly, we've run models, and there's too much inherent danger in venturing out beyond the fence to kill them. If we did that on a regular basis, we'd lose too many of our own. Look, I get that you're just finding this out now, but trust me, I've been grappling with this problem for three years. There was no solution before. There's even less of one now."

"Did you know what David was planning?"

"You mean with killing the power to the fence?"

"Yeah."

"No. I was sitting right here the night the fence went down. I called him. He wouldn't answer. He did it from his office and he locked me out of the system."

"So he didn't consult with you beforehand?"

"David and I haven't been on the greatest of terms these last few years."

"Why's that?"

Leven pushed his chair back from the controls and rolled across the floor.

"The David Pilcher you know wasn't the same man who hired me away from Lockheed Martin. The end of Wayward Pines has been coming for a long time, but David didn't want to face it. It's arrogance, I think, a refusal to admit that he missed this potential crisis. That he didn't foresee it and steer us all out of the way. Recently, he's become increasingly withdrawn. Erratic. Emotional. He killed his own daughter. That was the first major fracture. Then when you took control of the town and told the residents the truth, I think he just couldn't deal anymore. Said 'screw this' and hit self-destruct."

"So you're telling me it's over. We're all going to starve to death."

Leven smiled. "If the abbies don't get us first."

Ethan rose to his feet, watched the monitor scroll the list of depleted provisions like the writings of a doomsday prophet. He said, "You've got access to every database in the superstructure?"

"That is correct."

"Did you know a nomad just returned? Adam Hassler?"

"I heard rumblings of it."

"Do you have access to his file here?"

Leven tilted his head. "I don't really feel too hot about where this conversation is going."

"I want you to pull his file."

"Why?"

"Before Wayward Pines, Hassler and I used to work together. He was my supervisor in the Secret Service and the one who sent me here. I had no idea he was here until I saw him on the street a couple days ago. Come to find out, before Pilcher brought me out of suspension, Hassler was living here, and I don't think it's a coincidence. Something doesn't feel right."

Leven scooted back to the console array and went to work on the touch screens.

"And what is it exactly you'd like to know?" he asked.

Hassler's face appeared on the monitor, his eyes closed, skin pale—a post-suspension photo.

"How he came to be here."

"Oh." Leven quit typing, spun around in his chair. "I don't think I'm going to have that level of detail. You'll have to ask Pilcher himself."

Ethan stepped inside the cage, found David Pilcher eating his supper—some freeze-dried abomination from the winter reserves. The old man looked even older with the beginnings of a white beard fading in across his face, and as Ethan sat down across from him in the cramped cell, he wondered just how much rage simmered underneath the surface. Ethan had plenty of his own. He couldn't drive the image of those grieving families out of his mind, the sound of those shovels spearing into dirt. All that pain this one man's doing.

"That does not smell like Tim's cooking," Ethan said.

Pilcher glanced up.

Hard. Indignant. Defiant.

"It's like Satan shit on a plate. Must give you great pleasure."

"What?"

"Seeing me like this. Relegated to a cage that was built to hold a monster."

"I'd say it's serving its purpose perfectly."

"Thought you'd forgotten about me down here, Ethan."

"No, just been busy cleaning up the mess you made."

"The mess I made?" Pilcher laughed.

"Adam Hassler."

"What about him?"

"I hear that before I was brought out of suspension, Adam lived with my wife and son."

"As I recall, they were quite happy too."

"How did Adam Hassler come to be a resident of Wayward Pines?"

A touch of life crinkled in the corners of Pilcher's eyes.

"What does it matter now?" he asked.

"You do not want to fuck with me."

Pilcher set his plate aside.

Ethan said, "I'm told that he came here looking for me after my disappearance. And that you abducted him. That he woke up here just like I did. Like everyone in town did."

"Hmm. Interesting. Out of curiosity, who told you to come see me about this? Was it Francis Leven?"

"That's right."

"Is it possible that Francis also shared with you a piece of shocking news about our prospects going forward? And when I say 'our' I of course mean the human race."

"Tell me about Hassler."

"We're all going to be starving to death in a matter of years. Do you really think you're up to solving that problem, Ethan? Ready for that weight on your shoulders? What are you going to do? Put it to a vote? Look, I messed up. I realize that. But you need me. You all need me."

Ethan struggled onto his feet, started for the door.

"Okay, okay. At first, it was just a standard bribe," Pilcher said.

"What's a standard bribe?"

"Money. To buy Adam's silence for you, Kate Hewson, and Bill Evans. To shut down the investigation into your disappearances. But then something changed. He decided he wanted to come along with me and my crew. Be a part of our journey."

Ethan cocked his right arm back and punched the door.

Blood from his busted knuckles smeared across the steel.

He hit the door again.

"Between you and me," Pilcher said, "I always thought Hassler was an arrogant prick. I let him have one good year in Wayward Pines, and then I sent him out on a suicide mission beyond the fence. He never returned."

Ethan shouted for the guard.

"You need me," Pilcher said. "You know you need me. If something isn't done, we'll die out in a matter of—"

"It's not your concern anymore."

"Excuse me?"

The guard opened the door.

"How did you like your supper?" Ethan asked.

"What?"

"Your supper. How was it?"

"Terrible."

"Sorry about that, especially considering it was your last."

"What does that mean?"

"Remember when you asked me what was going to happen to you, and I said that's for the people to decide? Well. They decided. We took a vote a few hours ago, right after we finished burying all the people you murdered. And it's happening tonight."

Ethan walked out into the corridor as Pilcher screamed his name.

Late afternoon.

The sun already behind the cliffs.

The sky sheeted over with a uniform deck of clouds that seemed to threaten snow.

The power in town had yet to be restored, but still a handful of people had returned to their homes to begin the process of cleaning up, of trying to reassemble the pieces of a life that could never be made right again.

In the distance, the pile of abbies still burned.

Ethan wasn't sure what it was—maybe the lateness of the day, the darkening clouds, the cold, gray indifference of the towering cliffs— but Wayward Pines felt, possibly for the first time since he'd come here, like exactly what it was: the last town on earth.

He parked on the curb in front of his Victorian house on Sixth Street.

The vibrant yellow and the white trim struck him as off-key in light of the past few days.

They didn't live anymore in a world where life was to be colorful and celebrated. Life had become something you clung to, that you bit down hard on against the pain, like the rubber block in a session of electroshock therapy.

Ethan jarred open the Jeep's door with his shoulder and stepped down onto the street.

The neighborhood stood silent.

Joyless.

Tense.

There were no bodies visible, but a large bloodstain still marred the pavement nearby. It would take a day of solid rain to wash it away.

He stepped over the curb.

From the front yard at least, his house looked intact.

No windows broken.

No door smashed down.

He walked the flagstone path and stepped up onto the porch. The floorboards creaked.

He pulled open the screen door, pushed open the solid wood door.

It was dark and cold inside, and Adam Hassler sat in the rocking chair beside the dormant woodstove, looking like a wasted version of the man Ethan remembered.

"What the hell are you doing in my house?" Ethan's voice came out like a low growl.

Hassler looked over, his cheekbones and orbital rims pronounced from starvation.

He answered, "Believe me, I was just as surprised to see you."

Suddenly, they were on the floor, Ethan struggling to get his hands around Hassler's neck so he could squeeze the fucking life right out of him. He'd assumed that Hassler's emaciated state would make overpowering him simple, but the man's wiry strength was resilient.

Hassler torqued his hips and flipped Ethan onto his back.

Ethan swung, his fist glancing off Hassler's shoulder.

Hassler returned with a hard, stunning blow.

Ethan's world went pyrotechnic.

He tasted blood, felt it sliding down his face as his nose burned.

Hassler said, "You never knew what you had."

He threw another punch, but Ethan caught his arm at the elbow and jerked it the wrong way.

Hassler cried out as the ligaments stretched.

Ethan shoved him into the toppled rocking chair and scrambled up, looking for a weapon, something hard and heavy.

Hassler regained his feet, advanced in a boxer's stance.

Too dark in the living room for Ethan to see the punches coming.

Hassler connected a jab, then a hard right hook that might have turned Ethan's lights out if Hassler wasn't in such a weakened state.

Still, it snapped Ethan's neck and spun him ninety degrees as Hassler delivered a devastating kidney shot.

Ethan screamed out, stumbling back into the foyer as Hassler kept coming, calm and controlled.

"It's a mismatch," Hassler said. "I'm just better than you. Always was."

Ethan's fingers wrapped around the iron coatrack.

"I even loved your wife better than you could," Hassler said.

Ethan sent the hard, metal base arcing through the air.

Hassler ducked.

It punched a hole through the drywall.

Hassler charged, but Ethan caught him with an elbow to the jaw and the man's knees buckled. Ethan landed his first direct hit to Hassler's face, his cheekbone crunching under the blow, and it felt so goddamned good that Ethan hit him again. And again. And again. Hassler growing weaker, Ethan stronger, and with each punch the need to do more damage grew exponentially. The fear inside of him breaking out in a whirlwind of violence.

Fear of what this man could do.

Fear of what Hassler could take away from him.

Fear of losing Theresa.

Ethan let go of Hassler's neck and the man moaned on the floor.

Ripping the coatrack out of the wall, he clutched the metal in his hands and raised the heavy base over Hassler's head.

I'm gonna kill him.

Hassler looked up at him, his face a bloody mess, one eye already swollen shut and the other filling with the realization of what was coming.

He said, "Do it."

"You sent me here to die," Ethan said. "Was it for the money? Or so you could have my wife?"

"She deserves so much better than you."

"Did Theresa know that you orchestrated all of this so you could be with her?"

"I told her I came here looking for you and that I was involved in a car wreck. She was happy with me, Ethan. Truly happy."

For a long moment, Ethan stood over Hassler on the brink of caving in the man's skull.

Wanting to do it.

Not wanting to be the man who would.

He threw the coatrack across the living room and collapsed on the hardwood next to Hassler, his kidney throbbing.

"We're here because of you," Ethan said. "My wife, my son—"

"We're here because two thousand years ago you fucked Kate Hewson and destroyed your wife. If Kate had never transferred to Boise, she never would have come to Wayward Pines. Pilcher never would have abducted her and Bill Evans."

"And you never would have sold me out."

"Just to be clear, you'd be dead right now if I hadn't—"

"No, we'd have lived out our lives in Seattle."

"You call what you and Theresa had a life? She was miserable. You were in love with another woman. You want to sit there and tell me what I did was wrong?"

"You seriously just said that?"

"There's no right or wrong anymore, Ethan. There's only survival. I learned that in my three and a half years wandering around that hell beyond the fence. So don't look at me hoping to catch a glimpse of regret."

"It's kill or be killed now? That's where we're at?"

"We were always there."

"So why didn't you kill me?"

Hassler smiled, blood between his teeth.

"When you walked back to the superstructure from Kate's house last night? I was there. In the woods. It was dark, and it was just you and me. I had my bowie knife, the same one I killed abbies with in hand-to-talon combat you couldn't even fathom. You don't know how close I came."

Ethan felt something cold inch down his spine.

"What stopped you?" he asked.

Hassler wiped blood out of his eyes.

"I've been thinking a lot about that. I think it's because I'm not as hard as I'd like to be. See, in my head, I know there's no right or wrong, but my heart hasn't made that connection. My twenty-first-century hardwiring is too deep. Too institutional. My conscience intrudes."

Ethan stared at his old boss through the mounting darkness in the living room.

"Where does this leave us?" Ethan asked.

"The best moments of my life I lived right here. With Theresa. With your son."

Hassler groaned as he hoisted himself up into a sitting position against the wall.

Even in the low light, Ethan could see the man's jaw beginning to swell, Hassler's words now coming lopsided, garbled.

"I'll walk away," Hassler said. "Forever. One condition."

"You think you're entitled to a condition?"

"Theresa never hears about what really happened."

"You'd just be doing this so she goes on loving you."

"She chose you, Ethan."

"What?"

"She chose you."

Relief swept over him.

His throat ached with emotion.

"Now that it's over," Hassler said, "I don't want her to know. Respect that wish, and I'll make an impossible situation possible."

"There is another option," Ethan said.

"What's that?"

"I could kill you."

"Do you have that in you, old friend? Because if so, knock yourself out."

Ethan looked at the cold woodstove. Into the evening light coming through the windows. Wondered how this house could ever feel like home again.

"I'm not a murderer," Ethan said.

"See? We're both too soft for this new world."

Ethan got up. "You were out there for three and a half years?" he asked.

"That's right."

"So you know more about this new world than any of us."

"Probably so."

"What if I were to tell you that we couldn't stay in Wayward Pines any longer? That we needed to leave this valley and go someplace warmer, where crops could be grown? Do you think we'd have a chance?"

"Of surviving as a group on the other side of the fence?"

"Yeah."

"That sounds like mass suicide. But if we truly have no choice? If it's stay in this valley and die or take a chance heading south? I guess we'd have to find a way."

On his way up to the cafeteria, Ethan stopped again at the cage of the female abby. She was sleeping, curled up in a corner against the wall, thinner, frailer even than the last time he'd seen her.

One of the lab techs who worked in the abby holding facility moved past Ethan, heading toward the stairwell.

"Hey," Ethan called after him. The white-jacketed scientist stopped in the middle of the corridor, turned to face him. "Is she sick or what?" Ethan asked.

The young scientist flashed an ugly smile.

"She's starving to death."

"You're starving her?"

"No, *she* refuses to eat or drink."

"Why?"

The man shrugged. "No idea. Maybe because we made a bonfire out of all her cousins?"

The scientist chuckled to himself and continued down the corridor.

Ethan found Theresa and Ben at a corner table in the packed cafeteria. When she saw the bruises on his face, her eyes—tear-swollen and red—went wide.

"What happened?" she asked.

"Have you been crying?"

"We'll talk later."

Dinner consisted of packages of freeze-dried horror.

Lasagna for Ethan.

Beef Stroganoff for Ben.

Eggplant parm for Theresa.

All Ethan could think about was how much food this single meal was costing them.

One meal closer to nothing.

And no one had any concept of how fast the supplies were dwindling. Just took for granted that they could walk into this cafeteria, or down to the community gardens, or the town grocery, and find food.

Where would the civility go when it all ran out?

"You want to talk about what's going to happen later tonight, Ben?" Ethan asked.

"Not really."

"You don't have to go if you don't want to see it, sweetheart," Theresa said.

"I want to see it. This is his punishment for what he did, right?"

"Yeah," Ethan said, "and we have to do it, you understand, because there aren't courts anymore. No judges or juries. We have to watch out for ourselves, and that man hurt a lot of people. It has to be made right."

After dinner, Ethan sent Ben back to their quarters and asked Theresa to take a walk with him.

"So Hassler and I had it out," he said as they trudged up the stairs.

"Jesus, Ethan, what are you, in high school?"

Three doors down on the right-hand side of the Level 4 corridor, Ethan swiped his card at the reader and pulled open a heavy steel door.

They stepped onto a small platform.

Ethan said, "Hold onto the railing," and pressed the up arrow button.

The platform accelerated through the rocky tube at the speed of an express elevator.

Four hundred feet straight up.

When it finally shuddered to a stop, they stepped off onto a catwalk that ran for twenty feet until it terminated at a second steel door. Ethan swiped his card again. The lock buzzed. He pulled open the door and they moved outside into a wall of shocking cold.

"What is this place?" Theresa asked.

"Discovered it a few nights ago when I was up and couldn't sleep."

The clouds from earlier had blown out.

The stars were stunning.

Bright and sharp.

They stood in a path that had been carved three feet down into rock. On either side, the mountain fell away into oblivion.

He said, "I think people come up here to smoke, to get fresh air. It's the fastest way to see actual daylight without having to take the tunnel into town. They call this trail the sunroof."

"How far does it go?"

"All through these high peaks. If you stay with it, I'm told it winds down into the forest west of the cirque."

They strolled the knife-edge ridge.

Ethan said, "After we beat the shit out of each other, Adam and I talked."

"That sounds like borderline adult behavior."

"He said you chose me."

Theresa stopped, faced him.

He could feel the cold nibbling at the edges of his cheeks.

"It came down to a pretty simple choice for me, Ethan. Would I rather love or be loved?"

"What are you talking about?"

"Adam would do anything for—"

"So would I—"

"Will you listen? I told you I'd never been loved the way Adam loves me, and I meant that. But I've never loved anyone the way I love you. There are times I hated myself for it. Because I felt weak. When I wished I could've just hardened myself to you and walked away, but I could never do it. Even after Kate. It's like you've got some kind of hold on me. It's a precious thing, Ethan, and you'd better care for it. You've hurt me before. Badly."

"I know I've fucked up in the past. I know I haven't treated you the way you deserved to be treated."

"Ethan—"

"No, now it's my turn. I ruined things. Hell, I ruined everything. With my work. With Kate. With not dealing with my shit from the war. But

I'm trying, Theresa. Ever since I woke up in this town, I've been trying. Trying to protect you and Ben. Trying to love you the best that I possibly could. Trying to make the right choices."

"I know you have. I see it. I see what we could be. It's all I want. All I've ever wanted." She kissed him. "You have to promise me something, Ethan."

"What?"

"That you'll go easy on Adam. We all have to live together in this valley now."

Ethan stared down into Theresa's face, resisting the urge to tell her everything that man had done. He said, finally, "I'll try. For you."

"Thank you."

They walked on.

"What's wrong, honey?" she asked.

"Um, everything?"

"No, there's something more. Something new. You were weird at dinner."

Ethan looked into the canyon three thousand feet below. It was only a month ago he'd had his first encounter with the abbies down there, and as harrowing as that experience had been, at least he'd known hope then. He'd still believed the world was out there. That if only he could escape this town, these mountains, his family and his life would be waiting for him in Seattle.

"Ethan?"

"We're in trouble," he said.

"I'm aware."

"No, I mean we're not going to make it. As a species."

A meteor crossed the sky.

"Ethan, I've been here a lot longer than you have. It feels hopeless sometimes, and now more than ever, but we have everything we need in Wayward Pines."

"The food's running out," he said. "That stuff we ate tonight? Those freeze-dried meals? There isn't an endless supply, and once it's gone, we're not going to be able to grow enough food in this valley to get us through the long, hard winters. If we were farther south, we could make it work, but we're trapped in this valley. I'm sorry to tell you this, but I don't want to keep anything from you. No more secrets. I need you in my corner, because I don't know what to do."

"How long do we have?" Theresa asked.

"Four years."

"And then what happens?"

"And then we die."

HASSLER

He crossed the river on the east side of town, his legs numb by the time he stumbled out of the water and onto the far shore.

On all fours, he scrambled up through the pines that clung to the steepening hillside.

Up.

Up.

Up.

A hundred feet above town, the terrain went vertical, but he didn't stop, kept fighting his way up the cliff, higher and higher.

Climbing without fear.

Without care.

He couldn't believe he was actually scaling the suicide cliff. During that year he'd lived in town with Theresa, two people had ascended this stretch of rock and leapt to their deaths. There were plenty of other fatal options on the cliffs that surrounded Wayward Pines, but this particular precipice had the benefit of being the most sheer. No chances of accidentally bungling the jump and taking an unnecessary bounce off a ledge. If one made it to the top without falling, they could bank on an uninterrupted plummet into oblivion.

Hassler topped out five hundred feet above the valley on a long ledge.

He collapsed on the cold granite, his jaw throbbing, probably broken.

It was night and the town lay dark beneath him, paved streets glowing softly under the starlight.

His pant legs had frozen stiff.

As the chill set in, he thought about his life, and the peace he arrived at as he staggered onto his feet again was this: out of thirty-eight years, one had been magic. He'd lived in a canary-yellow house with the love of his life, and there hadn't been a day he'd woken up beside Theresa that he didn't know how good he had it.

He ached for more time with her, but the fact that he'd had any time at all . . .

It was enough.

Enough to cling to.

It took him a moment, but he found their home down there in the dark.

Fixing his gaze on it, he saw it not as it was, empty and dark, but rather as it had been in the soft, cool light of those summer evenings as he'd walk toward the front porch, toward everything he loved.

He stepped to the edge.

He wasn't afraid.

Not of death. Not of pain. He'd experienced enough agony on his nomadic mission for several lifetimes, and death was something he'd long since prepared for. If anything, it held, for him at least, the promise of peace.

He bent his knees to leap.

A noise pulled him out of the moment like a rip cord.

He turned, couldn't see much of anything in the darkness, but he realized it was the sound of someone crying.

He said, "Hello?"

The crying stopped.

A woman's voice asked, "Who's there?"

"Are you all right?"

"If I was do you think I'd be up here?"

"Yeah, I guess that's a fair point. Do you want me to come over?"

"No."

Hassler stepped back from the ledge, eased down onto the rock. "You shouldn't do this," he said.

"Excuse me? What the hell are *you* doing up here? I could tell you the same damn thing."

"Yeah, except I actually should be up here."

"Why? Because your life is so terrible too?"

"Do you want to hear my sob story?"

"No, I wanted to have jumped by now. I'd finally worked up the nerve when this asshole interrupted me. This is the second time I've climbed up here."

"What happened the first?" Hassler asked.

"It was daylight, and I hate heights. I chickened out."

"Why are you up here?" he asked.

"I'll tell you as long as you don't try to save me."

"Deal."

The woman sighed. "I lost my husband when the abbies came into town."

"Sorry to hear that. Were you two married in Wayward Pines?"

"Yes, and I know what you're thinking, but I loved him. I also loved this other man who's here. Crazy thing is we knew each other in our lives before. He's here with his wife and son, and when he came to tell me that my husband had been killed, I asked him if his family had survived."

"Had they?"

"Yeah, but you know what? There was a part of me, a bigger part than I want to admit, that was actually *sad* she had lived. Don't get me wrong, I miss my husband terribly, but I kept thinking . . ."

"If his wife had been killed, then the two of you . . ."

"Right. So on top of losing my husband, on top of the fact that I can't be with this man I love, it also turns out I'm a shitty human being."

Hassler laughed.

"Did you laugh at me?"

"No, I just think it's cute that you think *that's* horrible. Do you want to hear horrible?"

"Hit me."

"In my life before, I loved a woman, but she

was married to this guy who worked for me. I . . . arranged a chain of events so that her husband would be removed from the picture. See, I knew what this town was as it was being created two thousand years ago. I made certain this woman was abducted by David Pilcher, and then I volunteered to go into suspension so I could be with her when she woke up. We lived together in Wayward Pines, and she never knew she was here because of me. After a year, I was sent away on a mission beyond the fence. I was never supposed to return. Every day I was out there, it was the thought of her that kept me going, kept me breathing, putting one foot in front of the other. Against impossible odds, I made it back. I thought I'd be returning to her, to a hero's welcome. But instead, I find that her husband is here and the town has been destroyed."

Down in the darkness of the valley, tiny points of firelight had begun to gather on Main Street.

Watching them, Hassler said, "So I climbed up here to take my life. You thought about bad things. I did them. Does that shift things back into perspective?"

"Why are you up here?" she asked.

"I just told you."

"No, I mean, is it because you can't live with what you did? Or because you can't be with her?"

"Because I can't be with her. Look, I'm not going to stop loving her just because her husband's around. That's not the way the human heart works. I can't just amputate what I feel. It's not like we live in a big, wide world anymore where I can just move to another city, another state. There's no alternate life waiting out there for me to get on with. This is it. We're down to what? Two hundred fifty people? I can't avoid her, and what I feel for her has defined me for so long now, I don't know the person I'd be if I tried to walk away from it."

"I hear that."

"And the funny thing is, as bad as I am, I don't have it in me to murder her husband. Is there a fate worse than being halfway evil?"

For a moment, the only sound was the lonely whisper of wind blowing across the rock.

The woman finally said, "I know you, Adam Hassler."

"How?"

"I used to work for you."

"Kate?"

"Is life weird, or what?"

"I can leave you alone now if—"

"I'm not judging you, Adam."

He heard her get up, move toward him.

In a minute, she emerged out of the darkness, still just a shadow, and sat down beside him, their feet hanging off the edge together.

"Are your pants frozen too?" he asked.

"Yeah, I'm freezing my ass off. Do you think it

means something that you and I both climbed up here to jump on the same night?"

"What do you mean? Like, is the universe saying 'don't'? Can't we agree that the universe doesn't give a shit anymore, and probably never did?"

Kate looked over at him. "I don't care if we jump together or climb down together. But whichever it is, let's just not do it alone."

PILCHER

Someone grabbed his arm and pulled him down out of the truck. It was the first time he'd been outside in days, but he couldn't see anything through the black hood over his head.

"What's happening?" Pilcher asked.

The hood was ripped off.

He saw lights—fifty, sixty, maybe a hundred of them. Flashlights, torches, held by the residents of Wayward Pines, and by his own people from the mountain, all of whom surrounded him in a tight circle of bodies. As his eyes adjusted, he saw the buildings of Main Street looming above him, their facades and storefronts awash in fire-light.

Two men stood with him in the circle—Ethan Burke and Alan Spear, his head of security.

Ethan approached.

"What is this?" Pilcher asked. "You throwing a fête for me?"

He looked around at all the faces, hidden in shadow, distorted by firelight. Angry and intense.

"We took a vote," Ethan said.

"Who voted?"

"Everyone except you. A fête was on the table, but in the end it didn't feel right, putting you to death using the same self-policing approach you forced upon the citizens of Wayward Pines." Ethan took a step closer, his breath clouding in the cold. "Look at these people, David. Everyone here lost family, lost friends. Because of you."

Pilcher smiled against the rage.

The murderous, soul-melting rage.

"Because of me?" he asked. "That's hysterical." He stepped away from Ethan, moving out into the middle of the circle. "What else could I have *possibly* done for you people? I gave you food. I gave you shelter. I gave you purpose. I protected you from the knowledge you couldn't handle. From the harsh truth of the world that exists beyond the fence. And each of you had to do one thing. One! Goddamn! Thing!" He shrieked the words. *"Obey me."*

He caught the stare of a woman standing several feet away, the tears glistening as they ran down her cheeks.

So many tears in this crowd.

So much pain.

And once upon a time, he might have given a shit, but tonight he only saw ingratitude. Entitlement. Rebelliousness.

He screamed, "What more could I have fucking *done* for you?"

"They're not going to answer you," Ethan said.

"Then what is this?"

"They're here to walk with you."

"Walk where?"

Ethan turned to the nearest section of the crowd. "Would you all make way please?" As they parted, Ethan said, "After you, David."

Pilcher stared down the dark street.

He looked at Ethan.

"I don't understand."

"Start walking."

"Ethan—"

Someone shoved him from behind, and when Pilcher regained his balance, he turned to see Alan glaring at him with a lethal intensity.

"Sheriff said to go," Alan said. "Now *I'm* telling you, and if you can't make your legs work, we'll be happy to drag you by your arms."

Pilcher started walking south down Main Street, between the dark buildings, Ethan on one side, Alan on the other.

The crowd followed the three men like a vigil, and an uneasy silence descended. No one spoke. There was no sound but footsteps scraping the pavement and the occasional muffled sob.

He tried to hold it together, but his mind was frantic.

Where are they taking me?

Back to the superstructure?

To a place of execution?

They passed the Aspen House and then the hospital.

As everyone moved down the road into the

forest south of town, Pilcher realized what was going to happen.

He looked over at Ethan.

The fear sweeping through him like a shot of liquid nitrogen.

Somehow, he kept walking.

At the curve in the road, everyone stepped off the pavement and headed into the woods, Pilcher thinking, *I never even looked back, never got one last glimpse of Wayward Pines.*

A shallow layer of mist had pooled in the forest and the torchlights looked otherworldly cutting through it.

Like disembodied points of fire.

Pilcher was growing colder by the minute.

He heard the buzzing of the fence.

They were walking beside it.

Then they were standing at the gate. It had all happened so fast, as if no time had passed since they'd removed his hood in the middle of Main Street.

Ethan offered a small backpack to Pilcher.

"There's some food and water inside. Enough for several days if you last that long."

Pilcher just stared at the pack.

"You all didn't have the guts to actually kill me yourselves?" he asked.

"No," Ethan said. "Just the opposite actually. We all wanted it too much. We wanted to torture you. To let each person left standing take their pound of flesh out of you. Do you not want the pack?"

Pilcher grabbed it, slung the strap over his shoulder.

Ethan went to the control panel and punched in the manual power override.

The humming stopped.

The woods became quiet.

Pilcher looked at all his people. Those from town. Those from the mountain. The last human faces he would ever lay eyes upon.

"You ungrateful fucks! You'd all have died two thousand years ago if it wasn't for me. I created a paradise for you. Heaven on earth. I'm your God! And you have the audacity to kick God out of heaven!"

"I think you got your scripture wrong," Ethan said. "God didn't get exiled. It was the other guy."

Ethan opened the gate.

Pilcher looked at Ethan, long and hard, and then glared out at the crowd.

He crossed out of safety to the other side of the fence.

Ethan shut the gate.

Soon, the lines resumed their protective hum.

Pilcher watched as the crowd turned away from him, the flashlights and torchlights receding into the mist.

Then he was standing alone in the cold, dark forest.

He headed south until the hum of the fence became inaudible.

The starlight coming through the tops of the pines was insufficient to light his way.

When his legs became tired, he sat down against the trunk of a pine tree.

Far off, a mile or so away, an abby screamed.

Another one answered. Much, much closer.

And then another.

Pilcher heard the sound of footsteps.

Out there in the dark, something was running.

Running toward him.

ETHAN

At first light, Ethan drove out of the superstructure in one of the security team's Dodge Rams, his son riding beside him in the passenger seat.

Through the trees.

The boulders.

Then Ethan pulled onto the main road, heading south out of town.

At the hairpin curve, he turned off into the woods and steered down the embankment, weaving carefully between the trees.

When they reached the fence, Ethan turned parallel to it and drove until they arrived back at the gate.

He killed the engine.

The hum of the current moving through the barbed steel lines could be heard even from inside the truck.

"Do you think Mr. Pilcher is dead yet?" Ben asked.

"I have no idea."

"But the abbies will eventually get him, right?"

"That's a certainty."

Ben glanced back through the rear window into the bed of the truck. "I don't understand," he said. "Why are we doing this, Dad?"

"Because I haven't been able to stop thinking about that thing back there."

Now Ethan looked into the truck bed.

The female abby from the superstructure sat motionless in a plexiglass cage, staring out into the woods.

"It's strange," Ethan said. "The world belongs to them now, but we still possess something they don't have."

"What?"

"Kindness. Decency. That's what it is to be human. At our best at least."

Ben looked confused.

"I think this abby is different," Ethan said.

"What do you mean?"

"She has an intelligence, a gentleness I haven't seen in any of the others. Maybe she has a family she wants to see again."

"We should shoot her and burn her with all the rest."

"And what would that accomplish? Feed our anger for a few minutes? What if we did the opposite? What if we sent her out into her world with a message about the species that once lived in this valley? I know it's crazy, but I'm holding tight to the idea that a small act of kindness can have real resonance."

Ethan opened his door, stepped out into the forest.

"What do you mean?" Ben asked. "Like it

might change the abbies? Maybe more would become like her?"

Ethan walked around to the back of the truck, lowered the tailgate.

He said, "Species evolve. In the beginning, man was a hunter-gatherer. Communicated through grunts and gestures. Then we invented agriculture and language. We became capable of kindness."

"But that took thousands of years. We'll all be dead before that ever happens."

Ethan smiled. "You're right, son. It would take a long, long, long, long time."

He turned to face the abby. She sat peacefully in her cage, eyes still heavy from the sedative Ethan had ordered the scientists to administer.

Pulling his Desert Eagle from the holster, he climbed up into the bed, threw the locks on the cage, and eased the door open several inches.

Something between a purr and a growl rumbled in the abby's throat.

Ethan said, "I'm not going to hurt you."

He backed slowly away, climbed down out of the truck bed.

The abby watched him.

After a moment, she pushed the cage door open with her long left arm and crept out.

"What if it does something?" Ben asked. "What if it attacks—"

"She's not going to hurt us. She knows my

meaning." Ethan caught her eyes. "Don't you?"

He started toward the fence, the abby following sluggishly, several paces behind.

At the gate, he typed in the code for the manual power override, and waited as the bolts unlatched.

The fence went silent.

He shoved the gate open with his boot.

"Go on," Ethan said. "You're free now."

The abby watched him warily as she slunk past, squeezing herself through the opening, out into her world.

"Dad, you think we'll ever be able to live side by side with them?"

Ten feet out, the abby shot a glance back at Ethan.

Her head tilted.

She watched him for a beat, and he could have sworn she had something to say, her eyes brimming with intelligence and understanding.

There were no words.

But Ethan understood.

And all at once, it came to him.

"Yes," he said. "I do."

He blinked—

And she was gone.

Ethan sat with Theresa on one of the park benches, watching Ben, who stood in the middle of the field, staring up at the sky. A couple hundred feet above, a kite skirted along on the breeze. It had taken the boy several tries to get the kite up and out of the still air near the surface, but the patch of red was now a fixture against the perfect blue, twirling around on the currents.

It was a nice thing to sit and watch a child with a kite, and it was the first morning in days, maybe weeks, that didn't feel like winter.

"Ethan, that's insane."

"If we stay in this valley," he said, "we all die in a matter of years. There's not even a question. So why put it to a vote?"

"You let the *people* decide."

"What if—"

"You let the people decide."

"People get it wrong."

"That's true, but you have to figure out what kind of a leader you're going to be."

"I know what the right decision is, Theresa."

"So sell your idea to them."

"It's a hard sell. It's risky. And what happens if they make the wrong choice? Even you're on the fence."

"It's our wrong choice to make, honey. If you're willing to force this on people, then what was the point of ever telling them the truth about Wayward Pines?"

"I caused all of this," Ethan said. "All the death. The suffering and loss. I turned our lives inside out. Now I just want to fix it."

"Are you okay?"

"I'm terrified." She took his hand into hers. "You're not just asking me to trust the people with their fate. You're asking me to trust them with yours. With Ben's." Their son sprinted across the field, dragging the kite behind him, laughing. "The day I broke into the superstructure, Pilcher told me that I would come to understand the things he did. The choices he made."

"And do you now?"

"I'm starting to feel the weight that was on his shoulders."

"He didn't trust his people to make the right choices," Theresa said, "because he was afraid. But you don't have to be, Ethan. If you do what you know in your heart is right, if you give people the freedom to choose their own fate, their own destiny—"

"We could starve to death in this valley."

"That's true. But you won't have compromised your integrity. That's the only thing you really have to fear."

That night, Ethan stood where it had all begun, on the bare stage in the opera house, under the burn of the lights, with the last two hundred fifty people on the planet looking on.

"Here we are," he said to the crowd, "humanity at the end of the world. We're here right now because of the choice I made to tell everyone the truth about Wayward Pines. Don't think I've missed that. Many of you lost loved ones. We've all suffered. I'll live with my decision and what it cost for the rest of my life, but right now, it's time to consider the future. In fact, it's all I've been thinking about this past week."

The core group of Pilcher's inner circle sat together off stage left—Francis Leven, Alan, Marcus, Mustin—all watching him.

The quiet in the theater was absolute.

A coiled silence.

"I know we're all trying to figure out where we go from here," he said. "What happens next. What our lives might look like. We have some hard truths to face, and we need to face them together. Right now. Here's the first one. Our food is running out."

Gasps and whispers trickled through the crowd.

Someone shouted, "How long?"

"About four years," Ethan said. "Which brings us to the second hard truth. We can't stay in this valley. I mean, we could. Until the next fence failure. Until a winter comes like we've never imagined. Until the food supply is exhausted.

"Francis Leven is here from the superstructure and he can walk you all through the particulars, explain exactly why our lives are no longer sustainable in Wayward Pines.

"But I didn't drag you down here just to be the bearer of bad news. I also have a proposal for a new course of action. Something radical and dangerous and daring. A leap in the dark."

Ethan found Theresa in the crowd.

"To be honest, I debated even proposing this as a choice. A friend of mine recently said to me that sometimes we find ourselves in situations that are so life and death, one or two strong leaders need to call the shots. But I think we're all finished with having our lives controlled. I don't know how, but we're going to find our way through this. What it comes down to for me is that I'd rather us make bad decisions as a group, than to live in the absence of freedom. That was the old way. That was Pilcher's way.

"So all I ask is that you hear me out, and then we'll decide what to do. Together. Like free human beings."

ONE MONTH LATER

ETHAN

There were still moments like this one, with the power back on and the smell of Theresa's cooking emanating from the kitchen, when it all felt normal. Like it could've been any weeknight in Ethan's life before.

Ben upstairs in his bedroom.

Ethan sitting in the study, jotting down notes for tomorrow.

Out the window, in the evening light, he could see Jennifer Rochester's dark house. She'd been killed in the invasion and the recent cold had murdered her garden as well.

But the streetlamps were back on.

The crickets chirping through speakers in a distant bush.

He missed Hecter Gaither's piano, the sound of it coming through the radios in all the houses of Wayward Pines.

Would've loved to lose himself in the music one last time.

For just a moment, sitting in the oversize chair, Ethan shut his eyes and let the normalcy wash over him.

Tried to push their fragility out of his mind.

But it wasn't possible.

There was no coming to terms with the fact that

he was a member of a species on the verge of extinction.

It filled every moment with meaning.

It filled every moment with horror.

He walked into the kitchen to the smell of pasta boiling and spaghetti sauce thickening.

"Smells amazing," he said.

Moving up behind Theresa at the stove, he wrapped his arms around her waist and kissed the back of her neck.

"Last meal in Wayward Pines," she said. "We're going big tonight. I'm cleaning out the fridge."

"Put me to work. I can wash those dishes."

Stirring the sauce, she said, "I think it's probably all right to leave them."

Ethan laughed.

Right.

Of course it was.

Theresa wiped her eyes.

"You're crying," he said.

"I'm fine."

He took hold of her arm and turned her gently around, and asked, "What is it?"

"I'm just scared is all."

It was the last time they would sit together at this dinner table.

Ethan looked at Theresa.

At his son.

He stood.

He raised his water glass.

"I would like to say a couple words to the two most important people in my life." Already his voice trembled. "I'm not perfect. In fact, I'm pretty far from it. But there is nothing I wouldn't do to protect you, Theresa. And you, Ben. Nothing. I don't know what tomorrow holds. Or the day after. Or the day after that." He scowled against the gathering tears. "I'm just so grateful that we're together in this moment."

Theresa's eyes glistened.

As he sat down, shaken, she reached over and took hold of his hand.

It was the last night he would sleep on a soft mattress.

He and Theresa were intertwined, buried under a mountain of blankets.

The hour was late, but they were both still awake. He could feel her eyelashes blinking against his chest.

"Can you believe this is our life?" she whispered.

"Hasn't set in yet. Don't think it ever will."

"What if this doesn't work? What if we all die?"

"That's a real possibility."

"There's a part of me," she said, "that wants to

play it safe. Maybe we do only have four years left. So, what if we make them great? Savor every moment. Every bite of food, every breath of air. Every kiss. Every day we aren't hungry or thirsty or running for our lives."

"But then we definitely die. Our species is finished."

"Maybe that isn't such a bad thing. We had our chance. We failed."

"We have to keep trying. Keep fighting."

"Why?"

"Because that's what we do."

"I don't know if I'm cut out for this."

The door to their bedroom creaked open.

"Mom? Dad?" Ben's voice.

"What's up, buddy?" Theresa asked.

"I can't sleep."

"Come get in bed with us."

Ben crawled across the covers and burrowed down between them.

"Is that better?" Ethan asked.

"Yeah," Ben said. "Much better."

They all lay in the dark, no one talking.

Ben dozed off first.

Then Theresa.

And still Ethan couldn't sleep.

He sat up on one elbow and watched his family, watched them all through the night, until the sky lightened in the windows and dawn broke on their final day in Wayward Pines.

In every house throughout the valley, phones began to ring.

Ethan walked in from the kitchen holding a cup of black coffee and answered their rotary phone in the living room on the third ring.

Even though he knew the message that was coming, it still twisted his stomach up in knots as he held the receiver to his ear and listened to his own voice say, "People of Wayward Pines, it's time."

Ethan held the front door open for Theresa as she stepped out onto the porch carrying a cardboard box filled with framed photographs of their family—the only material possessions they had decided were worth taking.

It was a beautiful morning for leaving.

Up and down their block, other families were emerging from their houses, some carrying small boxes filled with their most precious belongings, others with nothing but the clothes on their backs.

The Burkes moved down the porch, through the front yard, and out into the street.

All the residents converged on Main and moved as one toward the forest on the southern outskirts of town.

Ethan spotted Kate up ahead, a backpack slung over her shoulder, walking with Adam Hassler.

Caught a stab of something he couldn't quite

wrap his head around, thinking maybe some emotions were too complex. But wherever this one fell on the color wheel, it was definitely in the neighborhood of nostalgia.

He let go of Theresa's hand and said, "I'll be right back."

Ethan caught up with his former partner as the group walked past the Aspen House.

"Morning," he said.

She glanced over, smiled. "Ready to do this?"

"It's insane, right?"

"Little bit."

Hassler said, "Hey, Ethan." A month in civilization had done wonders for the man. Hassler had put on enough weight to look almost like his old self again.

"Adam. How you guys holding up?"

"All right, I guess."

Kate said, "I feel like I'm about to get on this terrifying ride, you know? No idea where it's going."

They passed the hospital, Ethan thinking back to that first time he'd woken up to the smiling face of Nurse Pam. Those first days he'd wandered in a daze around this town, confused, still trying to call home and unable to reach his family. The first time he'd seen Kate, nine years older than she should've been.

What a journey.

Ethan looked at Kate. "It's going to get crazy

in a little while. I was thinking maybe we should say goodbye here."

Kate stopped in the middle of the road, the last residents of Wayward Pines moving past them. The way she smiled, the early sun in her face, eyes squinting—she looked like the Kate of old. Of Seattle. Of the worst and the best mistake he'd ever made.

They embraced.

Fiercely.

"Thank you for coming to look for me all those years ago," Kate said. "I'm sorry it ended up like this."

"I wouldn't change any of it."

"You did the right thing," she whispered. "Never doubt it."

Theresa reached them.

She smiled at Kate.

She went to Hassler and hugged him.

As they came apart, she asked, "Do you guys want to walk with us for a while?"

"We'd love to," Adam said. Ethan wondered, as he stood there with his wife, his son, his former mistress, and the man who had once betrayed him, *Is this what a family looks like in this new world?* Because no matter what had happened in the past, in this harrowing present, everybody needed everybody.

As the last of the crowd pushed on past them, they lingered where the main road out of

Wayward Pines entered the darkness of the forest.

Behind them, the town stood abandoned.

The morning sun glaring down against the streets.

The storefront glass shimmering on the west side of Main.

They took in all those picket-fenced Victorians.

The surrounding cliffs.

The turning aspen trees as the wind stripped their branches of the last golden leaves.

In this moment, it was so . . . idyllic.

Pilcher's brilliant, mad creation.

At length, they turned away and moved on down the road together, into the woods, away from Wayward Pines.

Ethan sat at the main console in the surveillance center, Alan on one side, Francis Leven on the other.

"What exactly is the point of this message?" Leven asked.

"In case someone stumbles across this place," Ethan said.

"I find that highly unlikely."

"Do you know what you want to say?" Alan asked.

"I wrote something down last night."

Alan's fingers danced across the touch screen.

"Ready when you are," he said.

"Let's do this."

"We're recording."

Ethan took the scrap of paper out of his back pocket, unfolded it, and leaned into the microphone.

He said his piece.

When he'd finished, Alan stopped the recording.

"Well said, Sheriff."

Above them, the bank of twenty-five monitors still streamed a rotating series of surveillance feeds from the valley.

The empty corridors of the hospital basement.

The empty hallway in the school.

The empty park.

Vacated homes.

Abandoned streets.

Ethan looked over at Francis Leven. "We ready?" he asked.

"All nonessential systems have been powered down."

"Everyone's prepped?"

"It's already underway."

As Ethan walked alone down the Level 1 corridor, the overhead lights winked out, one by one. When he reached the sliding glass doors that opened into the ark, he glanced back down the passage as the last light at the far end of the corridor went dark.

Already, it was colder, the heating and ventilation systems running on idle.

The stone floor of the great cavern was freezing against his bare feet.

It was frigid inside the suspension hub, just a few degrees above freezing. Masked by a blue-tinged fog, there was movement all around.

The machines hummed and ejected streams of white gas.

He pushed through the fog, turned a corner, and made his way between two rows of machines.

Men in white lab coats were helping the residents of Wayward Pines to climb into the suspension units.

He stopped at the machine at the end of the row.

The digital nameplate read:

KATE HEWSON
SUSPENSION DATE: 9/19/12
BOISE, ID
RESIDENT: 8 YEARS, 9 MONTHS, 22 DAYS

She was already inside.

Ethan peered through the two-inch-wide panel of glass that ran down the front of the machine.

Kate stared back at him, locked into her suspension unit.

She was trembling.

Ethan put his hand to the glass.

He mouthed, "It's going to be okay."

She nodded.

He hurried three rows down, threading his way through more people in white sleeping suits.

Theresa was kneeling down in front of Ben, holding him, whispering in his ear.

Ethan wrapped his arms around them, pulled his family in close.

Tears streamed.

"I don't want to do it, Dad," Ben cried. "I'm scared."

"I'm scared too," Ethan said. "We're all scared and that's okay."

"What if this is the end?" Theresa asked.

Ethan stared into his wife's green eyes.

"Then know I love you. It's time," Ethan said.

He helped Ben onto his feet, held the boy's arm as he stepped into his machine.

His son was shaking—from the cold, from the fear.

Ethan eased him down onto the metal seat.

Restraints shot out of the walls, locking around Ben's ankles and wrists.

"I'm so cold, Dad."

"I love you, Ben. I'm so proud of you. I have to shut the door now."

"Not yet. Please."

Ethan leaned in and kissed his forehead, thinking, *This could be the last time I ever touch my boy*. He stared into Ben's eyes.

"Look at me, son. Be brave."

Ben nodded.

Ethan wiped the tears from his cheek, stepped out of the suspension chamber.

"I love you, Ben," Theresa said.

"Love you, Mom."

Ethan gave the door to Ben's machine a nudge. It swung shut, and an internal locking mechanism triggered the seal.

Ethan and Theresa stared through the glass as the interior of Ben's chamber began to fill with gas.

They smiled through their tears as Ben's eyes closed.

Theresa turned to Ethan. "Tuck me in?" she asked.

He took her by the hand and walked her down to her machine. The door was already open, and she stared inside at the black composite seat, the armrests, the black tubing hanging from the inner wall, tipped with a large-gauge needle that would vacuum every drop of blood from her veins.

She said, "Oh Jesus Christ."

She climbed in and sat down.

The machine locked her in.

Ethan said, "I'll see you on the other side."

"You think we'll really get there?"

"Absolutely."

And then he kissed his wife like it was the last time he would ever touch her.

. . .

Climbing into his suspension chamber, Ethan thought of what he'd written down in his study last night, the words he'd recorded in the surveillance center.

Possibly the last recorded statement of human history.

The world is cruel. The world is hard, and in this valley, we lived at the mercy of the abbies. We lived like prisoners, and it went against every fiber of our being. Humanity is meant to explore; we're meant to conquer, to roam. It's in our DNA, and that's exactly what we're going to do.

He sat down in the seat.

It's going to be a long journey, and when we reach our destination, there's no telling what we'll find.

The restraints locked around his ankles.

I'm afraid. We all are.

His wrists.

What kind of a world awaits us on the other side of this long sleep? To some extent, it doesn't matter. Because the residents of Wayward Pines will face it together. No secrets. No lies. No kings.

The door to his own chamber clanged shut and locked.

We've all said our goodbyes. We all know this could be the end, and we've made as much peace with that fact as we can.

The pressurized hiss of releasing gas was accompanied by a woman's voice, computerized and strangely comforting.

She said, "Please begin breathing deeply. Smell the flowers while you can."

They say time heals all wounds . . . Well, we've got plenty of it . . . Enough time for empires to rise and fall. For species to change. For the world to become a kinder place.

The gas smelled like lavender and lilac, and the moment he breathed it in, he felt his consciousness being kicked out from under his feet.

So we all embark wondering what lies over the horizon, what's around the next bend. And isn't that, in the end, what drives us?

His eyelids began to lower, and he conjured up the faces of his wife, his son.

We have hope again.

Took Theresa and Ben with him, down into that long, long sleep.

For now, the world belongs to the abbies, but the future . . .

The future could be ours.

EPILOGUE

Seventy thousand years later, Ethan Burke's eyes slammed open.

WAYWARD PINES

ACKNOWLEDGMENTS

Deepest gratitude to David Hale Smith, Richard Pine, Alexis Hurley, everyone at Inkwell Management, and to my West Coast fighters, Angela Cheng Caplan and Joel VanderKloot. You're an extraordinary team, and I'm blessed to have you behind my books.

The folks at Thomas & Mercer and Amazon Publishing—Alan Turkus, Daphne Durham, Jeff Belle, Kristi Coulter, Danielle Marshall, Gracie Doyle, Andy Bartlett, Sarah Tomashek, Reema Al-Zaben, Philip Patrick, Tiffany Pokorny, Nick Loeffler, and Jodi Warshaw—are as fearless a group as I've ever had the pleasure of working with. I'm thrilled to be on this ride with you.

Thanks to Jacque Ben-Zekry, who edited the hell out of this book and stopped it from sucking in a thousand different ways.

And to Michelle Hope Anderson for a terrific copyedit.

Ann Voss Peterson, Joe Konrath, Marcus Sakey, and Jordan Crouch offered superb feedback and helped me to take this book to another level.

And lastly—most importantly—thank you to my beautiful, wonderful family.

xoxoxoxo

ABOUT THE AUTHOR

Blake Crouch is the author of over a dozen bestselling suspense, mystery, and horror novels. His short fiction has appeared in numerous short story anthologies, *Ellery Queen's Mystery Magazine*, *Alfred Hitchcock's Mystery Magazine*, *Cemetery Dance*, and many other publications. Much of his work, including the Wayward Pines series, has been optioned for TV and film. Blake lives in Colorado. To learn more, follow him on Twitter or Facebook, or visit his website, www. blakecrouch.com.

Books are produced
in the United States
using U.S.-based
materials

Books are printed
using a revolutionary
new process called
THINKtech™ that
lowers energy usage
by 70% and increases
overall quality

Books are durable
and flexible because
of Smyth-sewing

Paper is sourced
using environmentally
responsible foresting
methods and the
paper is acid-free

Center Point Large Print
600 Brooks Road / PO Box 1
Thorndike, ME 04986-0001 USA

(207) 568-3717

US & Canada:
1 800 929-9108
www.centerpointlargeprint.com